THE MARRIAGE INHERITANCE

When Caroline Adams arrives at Rafe Worthington's Northumberland castle, she finds her holiday cottage is uninhabitable. Rafe offers her accommodation in return for playing his fiancée, to foil his scheming cousin Jenna's plans for the castle. Caroline agrees, but then she confesses all to Rafe's great aunt. Jenna's scheming is exposed and Caroline runs back to London, but Rafe follows her, prepared to give up the castle for the woman he loves.

MICHELLE STYLES

THE MARRIAGE INHERITANCE

Complete and Unabridged

LINFORD
Leicester

First published in Great Britain in 2005

First Linford Edition
published 2006

British Library CIP Data

Styles, Michelle
    The marriage inheritance.—Large print ed.—
Linford romance library
    1. Imposters and imposture—Fiction
    2. Love stories 3. Large type books
    I. Title
    823.9'2 [F]

    ISBN 1–84617–379–5

Published by
F. A. Thorpe (Publishing)
Anstey, Leicestershire

Set by Words & Graphics Ltd.
Anstey, Leicestershire
Printed and bound in Great Britain by
T. J. International Ltd., Padstow, Cornwall

This book is printed on acid-free paper

1

Caroline Adams knew the instant she pressed the doorbell that it was a mistake, another in the long line of today's disasters.

The notice instructing visitors to go to the estate office was directly in front of her nose. For an instant she contemplated running, but the bell still echoed and the door creaked.

She crossed her fingers and hoped that some aged retainer would open the door. Haydon Castle had that sort of air to it with its sandcastle look, battlements and large, oak doorway. The owner was probably some aged lord with a red face and booming voice.

She saw the door swing open and parted her lips intending to make some sort of apology but found herself staring at the man who stood in the doorway of the castle. Instead of the

1

expected servant, one of the most attractive men Caroline had seen in a long time stood before her eyes, tall, broad-shouldered but slender with cheekbones to die for. She tilted her head to meet his eyes and noticed that the intense green sweater matched his eyes exactly.

'Can I help you?'

His voice matched his looks — deep and well-spoken, a voice that dripped prestige and good schooling.

After a heartbeat, she dropped her eyes and tried to get a grip on her emotions. Standing staring as if she was a star-struck schoolgirl faced with her favourite pop idol was not going to get her any quicker to the cottage she'd rented. She shook her head trying to clear it. Nerves, it must be her nerves, acting up after this morning's trauma — this sudden loss of an ability to form a meaningful sentence.

'Can I help you?' he asked again.

Caroline swallowed hard, put down the cat carrier she was grasping and held out her right hand.

'I'm Caroline Adams,' she said and was greeted with a blank look from Mr Gorgeous. 'The person who is renting Echo Cottage for the next two weeks. I've come to collect the keys. The confirmation letter said I was to collect the keys from the estate office at Haydon Castle. I've walked around the castle three times, but there didn't seem to be a sign pointing to it.'

The man pointed to the small sign clearly indicating the direction to the estate office. Caroline felt the blood rush to her face. She bit her lip to keep the torrent of apologetic words from tumbling out. She traced the toe of her trainer along a crack in the stone step, wishing the earth would open up and swallow her.

'Thanks, thanks very much. Sorry to have troubled you.'

'Wait a minute,' the man called after her. 'Did you say Echo Cottage?'

She stopped with a sudden hope of redemption. Maybe he would help after all. Maybe she hadn't made a complete fool of herself.

'I'm renting Echo Cottage for two weeks. The letter said to arrive between three and half past six. I know it's only ten to three so I hope I'm not too early.'

'Didn't someone telephone you earlier today?'

Her heart plummeted. Not another complication!

After being woken up at four-thirty this morning with half the ceiling falling in, courtesy of the do-it-yourself upstairs madman's attempted removal of a wall, yesterday's letter in the post about the redevelopment of the warehouse where her company was located and the bank manager's phone call late yesterday afternoon about his tentative refusal of her request for funds for the expansion of the business, all she needed was more problems.

'I've been out of contact for most of the day.'

'I'm sure Mrs Tomlinson tried.'

The man looked apologetic and her heart sank still further.

'I'm incredibly sorry about this but the cottage isn't ready.'

She looked at him in stunned disbelief. She refused to believe her ears. So many disasters could not happen in one day. She swallowed hard and tried again.

'I booked this holiday only last week. I've driven all the way up from London.'

'The previous tenant left the bath running last night. It overflowed and ran down the walls of the sitting-room. There is no way the cottage is habitable. I'm terribly sorry.'

Her earlier thoughts about the gorgeousness of the man vanished. He was being arrogant and overbearing. A few words of apology and a falsely contrite manner weren't good enough, and he had to know it.

'Look here, mister, the word, sorry, is not good enough. I have driven over five hundred miles today, expecting a warm cottage, a hot meal and a comfortable place to sleep, and what do I find through no fault of my own? A hovel. And you talk to me about slight inconveniences. I paid in advance. What do you expect me to do? Simply say I'm sorry to have troubled you and turn around and drive back through some of the worst traffic known to mankind?'

The man crossed his arms across his broad chest, and tilted his head to one side as if assessing her story.

'I'd offer to put you up in one of our other cottages, but it's the start of the high season for holidays, and I'm afraid they're all let. I'd hoped Mrs Tomlinson might be able to reach you and explain the situation before you left wherever it is you live, but it obviously didn't happen.'

'I asked for a solution to my problems, not a recounting of the whole history. Perhaps, if I could see the owner . . . '

Caroline fumbled in her purse for her confirmation letter.

'Here it is. I would like to speak to Mr Rafe Worthington, please.'

'Speaking,' the terse reply came.

She gulped, but recovered her poise in an instant.

'Well, then, Mr Worthington, I'd like to know what you are going to do about sorting out this mess.'

'Of course, I, on behalf of Northumbria Country Cottages, will do my best to sort out your problems, but miracles are beyond me, I'm afraid. If you follow me, please.'

Caroline followed the man into the castle, past several suits of armour, large dark wooden chests and a number of paintings, into the well-furnished oak-panelled study. It had a faint musty smell of cedar wood, leather and coal fires and reminded her of the solicitor's office where the dry-as-dust solicitor had read out loud her parent's will, and informed her there was very little money left, certainly not enough to attend university as she had planned.

The old, empty feeling in the pit of

her stomach that started whenever she thought about that time was back. She swallowed rapidly and tried to push it away. She was a successful businesswoman of twenty-seven, not a schoolgirl of seventeen. She refused to break down in tears in front of a stranger, not a chance.

She sat down on the edge of a large red velvet-covered oak chair opposite the desk. Lowering her gaze to her hands clasped in her lap, she noticed a rather large hole in the knee of her jeans and hurriedly put the cat carrier over it. Luckily, his attention appeared to be caught by the papers on the desk. When he glanced up, she smiled.

'Now, precisely how long were you planning on staying in the area?'

Rafe tried to remember everything Mrs Tomlinson had told him about the situation when she left this morning, but he hadn't paid much attention. He'd been too concerned with sorting out the final details of his relatives' visit to give the potential problems of clients much thought. Besides, Susan Tomlinson had promised to keep trying to contact the woman.

The woman in question snapped her head up and stared back at him, her vivid blue eyes watery but defiant. He thought about offering a handkerchief but decided against it. She'd probably take it as an insult to her pride.

'Two weeks. I've the confirmation letter here.'

She rummaged in her purse for a second and then held out a piece of paper, nearly toppling over the large carrier she held on her knee.

Rafe glanced over the letter. It was the standard confirmation Susan Tomlinson always sent out, setting out times, payment details. Ms C. Adams was correct. She had rented the cottage for two weeks, starting today. He'd half-hoped that the days had been mixed up somehow. The easiest solution was to put her up somewhere else. He reached for the telephone.

'Would you prefer to stay at a hotel

or a bed-and-breakfast? There are a number of good ones in the area. We can put you up in a room and then when a cottage becomes available . . . '

Rafe paused and flipped through a large calendar. Ms Adams with her problem was precisely what he didn't need right now. He had about twenty-five minutes to solve this and get rid of her before his fiancée showed up.

'Fell House becomes vacant in two days' time. It's in a higher price band than Echo because it is a slightly larger house and has a microwave and dishwasher. You can stay there, at no extra charge. I'm terribly sorry about this, Miss . . . Ms Adams.'

'There's a problem about staying at a hotel or a bed and breakfast.'

'Problem? What sort of problem?'

Beyond offering her alternative accommodation, he didn't have time to deal with this. Rafe leaned back in his chair and took a closer look at the person sitting opposite. How could he describe Ms Adams? Urchin was probably the best word considering her smooth, sun-kissed hair and grubby clothes but there was a certain grace and dignity about the way she held her head. And her voice — besides being pleasant to the ear, it held an authority that no urchin would have. She was a woman who was used to being in charge, not pleading for a favour.

'I have my cat with me,' she said at last in a small voice.

'You travel with your cat?' Rafe asked, his eyes wide in astonishment.

'There was no-one to leave him with. Margo would forget to feed him and Jules was going away for the weekend. The flat was uninhabitable anyway. It seemed the most sensible thing to do.'

Her bottom lip trembled as he put a hand to his brow and closed his eyes briefly. Not tears. Anything but feminine tears. How he wished he hadn't given Susan the afternoon off. Nothing the clients did fazed her and she always seemed in complete control of the situation. On the other hand, he was very close to losing his temper with this person. He fought to keep the incredulity out of his voice.

'Why didn't you put him in a cattery? Isn't that what they are for?'

'Bertram hates catteries.'

'You allow your cat to make your decisions for you?'

The woman's face flushed and her eyes flashed.

'It's not that simple.'

'Things rarely are.'

To buy time, Rafe ruffled through a few bits of paper. The last thing he needed was a stand-up fight with a mad woman who travelled with her cat.

'I'm not sure Northumberland Country Cottages allows cats.'

'Bertram is a very well-trained cat,' she said before he'd finished, her blue eyes pleading with him for understanding. 'And never scratches the furniture. I did check your brochure. It said that one dog was allowed, and Bertram is

12

like a lap-dog almost. Anyway, he's here.'

She held up the cat carrier for closer inspection. He looked at the cat, and then back at the cat's owner.

'Are you sure that this creature is a cat, not a mountain lion in disguise?'

The woman laughed. There was something about the laugh that made Rafe want to hear it again.

'Bertram's a Norwegian Forest cat, a gentle giant. He's great company and very clean. Only I can't see a hotel proprietor allowing a cat in a room.'

The owner of the castle gave a snort that might have been a suppressed chuckle and Caroline felt more embarrassed than ever. What seemed like a good idea at six o'clock this morning seemed like a foolish one at over seven hours later. Where was her usual good sense? It had been madness to bring Bertram. She should have thought.

'There are two catteries around here, I believe.' His voice was kinder, less impatient. 'There's a good one in the next village. Perhaps you could leave him there.'

Caroline put the carrier back down on her lap and wriggled her fingers through the bars at Bertram who rubbed his head against them.

'Catteries require immunisation papers. I don't have Bertram's papers with me, and even if I did, I told you, Bertram hates catteries.'

'That's . . . '

The ring of the phone interrupted his answer.

'Worthington here,' he said. 'Where are you? London? But I thought you were supposed to be arriving at half past one? Not coming? Your boyfriend's going to marry you? Yes, I understand completely. Not a problem, don't worry, I'll manage.'

He hung up the phone with a blank expression on his face, staring off into the distance. Caroline waited for him to continue.

'A problem?'

The sound of her voice caused his

head to jerk up and his eyes to focus. He gave a brief smile.

'Today seems to be that sort of day. Getting back to your accommodation difficulty.'

He picked up a pen and started to make some notes, then paused and looked more closely at Caroline. She shifted under the intensity of his gaze.

'Do you have another idea? Somewhere my cat and I could stay together?' she asked to fill the gap of silence.

His hand stopped in mid-air, and his eyes lit up with a bright green light. Caroline revised her opinion of him again. Maybe he was human after all.

'I think I may have the solution to your problem, to both our problems. It's quite straightforward, but it has potential, definite potential.'

A slight smile played on his lips as Caroline crossed her arms and leaned back in her chair.

'Anything that doesn't involve a

significant amount of driving would be a start.'

'You can be my fiancée for the weekend.'

'Your what?'

She nearly dropped Bertram's carrier, and made a wild grab as it slid towards the floor, catching the carrier just before it touched the ground. She looked more closely at the man sitting behind the desk, and tried to make sense of what he said. Her ears must have been affected by the crash when the ceiling fell in this morning.

This man, who seemed to have everything going for him — looks, a big house, probably lots of girlfriends, personality — wanted her to play at being his fiancée? It didn't make any sort of logical sense.

'My fiancée,' he started again, slowly as if speaking to a dim-witted child. 'You needn't look at me like that. It isn't as if I asked you to be my mistress. You have a problem and I have a different problem. I think I've found the solution to both our problems. You need somewhere to stay with your cat for the weekend, and I suddenly have need of a fiancée.'

2

'A fiancee?' Caroline repeated, staring at the man seated behind the desk, a smile curving on his lips. 'How can you suddenly need a fiancée, and only for a weekend? Normally people make some sort of advanced arrangements for such a thing.'

'It's a long story.'

Rafe shrugged and looked directly at her. Despite her earlier reservations, Caroline felt her heart turn over.

'But the woman I thought I was going to marry in about two weeks' time has dumped me.'

Heartless, that's what he is, heartless! If she'd just been dumped by her fiancé, she wouldn't be sitting there, showing no emotion, offering to marry a complete stranger.

'It still doesn't mean you need a fiancée immediately,' she pointed out.

'These things happen. I'm sure you'll find a nice girl soon. Getting married on the rebound to the first girl in the vicinity is not a good idea at all.'

Her eyes flicked between the door and her chair. She tightened her grip on the cat carrier, weighing up the chances. If she picked up Bertram quietly, she might be able to make it, before he could get around the desk.

'I don't need a nice girl soon. I need her in an about an hour's time.'

Maybe he was some sort of weird modern-day Bluebeard. Maybe this idea of a holiday in Northumberland had been a mistake.

'Uh . . . look, I'm really sorry about all this, but I can find my own accommodation. Marriage to anyone, let alone a stranger, is simply not in my plans. I'm sorry but you'll have to think of something else.'

Mr Perhaps Bluebeard stood up and came over to Caroline's chair. He was so close she could see the faint stubble on his jaw.

'I haven't explained it very well, have I? I need to show my great aunt and my cousin that I'm getting married, that I'm fulfilling the terms of my great uncle's will. I'm betting that my cousin, when faced with defeat, will be unable to stop herself from losing her temper. When she loses her temper, everything will come out, including her and her new husband's plan to turn any portion of this estate they can get their hands on into a holiday centre.'

Caroline stood up and held the carrier defensively in front of her.

'I don't understand why you need a fiancée. If you know so much about your cousin's plans, why don't you simply expose them to your aunt?'

'It isn't that easy. I lack concrete proof. My cousin could say I was trying to get out of fulfilling my duty.'

'I don't understand what a fiancée has to do with whether or not your cousin can buy part of this estate.'

Rafe stared in disbelief at the woman clutching her cat carrier as if it were a life preserver. What hadn't he explained? His gaze swept round the study, taking in all the familiar furniture from his boyhood and finally coming to rest on the portrait of his great uncle. There was no way he was going to let this room be turned into a rumpus room or whatever other themed room his cousin might devise, not while there was a modicum of hope. Unfortunately, this woman, such as she was, was his only hope.

He tried again, taking the time to enunciate each word.

'When I inherited the castle and the estate nearly seven years ago, my great uncle's will stated specifically that I had to be married at the end of seven years otherwise my great aunt would inherit the castle and its contents. Until recently she's been happy to leave me to run the estate and let me find a wife in my own good time, but lately she's started talking about the need to provide an heir for the castle.'

'I'm sorry, but I still don't understand why you need a fiancée.'

'The sole purpose of this visit by my cousin is to expose me as a liar. Six months ago when Jenna first started her campaign, I invented a fiancée, never dreaming that she'd be required to show herself. Other than my great uncle's funeral, Aunt Alice has only been able to come up to Northumberland three times in the last seven years. It wasn't until Jenna called my bluff, so to speak, that a real live fiancée became a necessity.'

'But you said your fiancée dumped you.'

'The woman who was going to portray my fiancée called to say that she's made up with her boyfriend, and doesn't need to marry me after all.'

'I'm not so desperate for a place to lay my head that I'm going to marry a complete stranger.'

Rafe drummed his fingers.

'I doubt it will come to that. Jenna hates being thwarted in anything. She used to have screaming fits when I beat her at any game as a child. When she goes, she lets everything hang out. One good temper tantrum in my aunt's hearing and her dream of turning this castle into a holiday pleasure palace will be over.'

'Why do you think she has designs on your castle? Can't you simply confront her and your aunt with your suspicions? Surely you have some proof even if it is not in writing. There must be something that made you suspicious.'

'No concrete proof,' he repeated, shaking his head. 'Only a feeling in my bones. Ever since childhood, Jenna has referred to this place as a heap of rocks, but suddenly within a few months of marrying Howard Steel . . . '

'Do you mean Howard Steel of Steel Developments?' Caroline asked, thinking back to the letter she received yesterday morning, and her trip to the planning department. The company planning to redevelop the warehouse where she had based her company for the last six years was Steel Developments!

'Do you know him?'

'Only by reputation, but I've seen some of his work. It's very sleek and modern. His developments seem to push the boundaries of what is acceptable, but they stay within the law. I don't think he cares much for the planning laws.'

She thought of her talk with the planning officer who, in the end, said that there was little they could do — Steel Developments had paid attention to all details. In her car was a whole pile of papers on planning law that she was to pore over. There had to be some way of fighting this company or at least making life so uncomfortable for them that they went away.

'Precisely, and I believe that he intends to try to develop part of the estate into a holiday centre with the Roman Wall as its theme. I love this land and the people who farm it, as does my aunt. She grew up in the area, and believes strongly that we are the custodians for future generations. She is very proud of the Worthington connection to this land. At the moment, Jenna is pushing all the right buttons, saying all the things my great aunt wants to hear.'

'I still don't see why you need a fiancée. Just confront your cousin.'

'Please pay attention.' Rafe slapped his hand on his forehead. 'It has to do with great uncle's will. My great aunt has the power to sell the castle, if I'm not married within seven years of my uncle's death.'

He held up a hand silencing her protest.

'My dear aunt is also a romantic. My new plan is to introduce you as my fiancée, and after a suitable time, I'll say we broke up, and she'll allow me more time to recover. During that time, one of two things will happen. Either Jenna and Howard will reveal their plans or I will meet the woman I want to marry, the woman who is right for this castle.'

Caroline stared at him in shock. She was surprised that she hadn't picked up the cat carrier and walked out without a backward glance. Ice water, that's what ran in his veins. No wonder he'd had trouble finding a wife. Most women wanted warmth and affection, not some Victorian-style arranged marriage.

She was about to wish him good luck at finding a paragon of virtue when Bertram gave a small miaow forcibly reminding her of her own problem. She needed to find somewhere to sleep tonight. No way could she face another long drive. Her head started to pound at the thought.

She traced a finger along the top of the cat carrier.

'I'd only have to play at being your fiancée for the weekend?'

'Until Jenna and Aunt Alice leave or until Jenna reveals her plans.'

For half a minute she was tempted, anything not to have to face more driving, but in reality, it wasn't going to work, and when it didn't work, she'd be worse off than before — an emotional as well as a physical wreck.

'Look, the scheme is crazy. You don't know the first thing about me. I could be anybody. I'm just someone who rented a cottage from you.'

'Caroline, it is Caroline, isn't it? You need a place to stay for the weekend, a place that will take in your rather large cat. I am offering you that place. You tell me where you are going to find a better offer than this one. All you need to do is tell a few white lies.'

His face softened.

'I won't leave you floundering. It is in my best interest this works.'

It was the eyes again, doing strange things to her insides. Her eyes were drawn to his bow-shaped mouth. She wondered what it would be like to feel his mouth on hers. She felt her face grow hot, and looked away from his gaze. She rubbed her temple. She must be more tired than she imagined, having thoughts like that.

He was probably used to women falling all over him at the slightest hint. She clenched her jaw. This was one woman who would remain aloof.

'When you put it that way, I don't see how I can refuse, do you?'

'Thank you, I really appreciate what you're doing,' Rafe said, his voice sending shivers along her spine.'

'You will find I'm the most reasonable of fiancées.'

Two could play that sort of flirting game, she decided on impulse.

'Then permit me to seal our engagement with a kiss,' Rafe murmured, covering the distance between them in two strides.

His arms circled her, holding her gently. His scent filled her nostrils with an intoxicating combination of outdoors, cashmere and a hint of aftershave, just before his lips captured hers. For one wild second, she wondered if he had read her mind. Giving into impulse, she encircled her arms about his waist and tilted her head back. Rafe stepped back.

'Do you kiss all the men you meet like that or am I simply lucky?'

How dare he make such an assumption!

'I want to be a fiancée in name only. I don't jump into bed with every man I meet,' Caroline said, trying to get her breath back.

'Is that a challenge?'

'Don't be ridiculous.'

'It certainly sounded like a challenge.'

She picked up the cat carrier and held it in front of her to ward off any further demonstrations. Her legs felt like jelly but she managed to stagger a few steps backwards.

'Whatever gave you the idea that I might think otherwise? I'd hardly need to go through this play-acting if I only wanted to seduce you, now, would I? There are many other ways, much pleasanter ways.'

He reached out a hand and traced a path along the line of her jaw, sending another shiver down the back of her spine.

'I've agreed to be your fiancée, not your plaything.'

She brushed away his hand. His face was expressionless, but the corners of his mouth twitched.

★　★　★

Caroline paced the bedroom for the fourth time since Rafe had shown her where she was going to stay. A little over twenty-four hours ago, she'd been leading her normal life, preparing for her first holiday in ages. Now, she was a wreck!

Usually she was calm and collected, the efficient unemotional one of the team, but her hands were shaking and her mind spinning. Still, she supposed, looking around the room with its floral wallpaper and curtains, and the delicately-patterned oriental carpet, there were worse places to have to spend time.

The window was half-open and a light breeze fluttered through, bringing with it the smell of damp earth, freshly-mown grass and the slight perfume of wild flowers. Caroline breathed in deeply, savouring it. It was very different from the exhaust-ridden smell of London.

She clambered down and grabbed her small sketchbook, and started to draw the scene. This was precisely the sort of inspiration she needed to start her follow-up to the myths' theme of the cross-stitch book that had sold so well last year. She'd recently signed a contract with one of the major needlework kit manufacturers in the United States and the early signs were the kits were going to be just as successful over there. However, this newfound prosperity wouldn't last long if she didn't keep producing work to the same standard.

She'd thought that success on this scale would be the crowning moment, that all her problems would be solved if only Adams' Stitchery was a success. However, her success didn't taste sweet. Instead of paradise, success had brought more problems, more responsibility and above all more decisions, until she found even the smallest decision fraught with trauma. It was after bursting into tears when a shipment of buttons was late that she knew a break, and this time a long holiday instead of her usual twenty-four-hour breaks, was needed.

Caroline added another row of scales to the dragon's back and a small tongue of flame to its mouth as a late-afternoon breeze touched her cheek. It broke her concentration, and she closed the window. She held the sketch an arm's length away and examined it critically. She then tried drawing the dragon from another angle.

The soft knock made her jump and caused the pencil to slip so she drew a line down the side of the dragon's face. She put the sketchbook down and padded over to the door.

Ms Adams seemed completely at her ease, Rafe thought looking the woman up and down as she opened the door. There was something about the way her hair formed a halo around her head that made him want to reach out and touch it. He cleared his throat.

'I thought you ought to have a ring.'

He handed her a small black box and listened to the slight gasp as she opened it. The ring, two sapphires intertwined with a series of seven small diamonds, sparkled in the sunshine. When Caroline put it on, it looked as if it had been made for her. She turned her hand this way and that, watching the stars move in the blue stones. With a sigh, she slipped it off.

'I can't wear this.'

'Why not? If you are going to be my fiancée, you'll have to look the part. They'll expect to see a ring.'

'Yes, but this is obviously a family heirloom.'

She held the box out to him.

'It's what Aunt Alice will expect to see.'

Rafe tried to contain his annoyance. Time was running out and the girl wasn't co-operating. They had to work together if this scheme stood any chance of succeeding.

'If you wear anything else, she'll suspect something is amiss. Every Worthington bride has worn that ring for one hundred and fifty years.'

Caroline allowed Rafe to slide the ring back on to her finger.

'It's very beautiful. Your mother must have loved it very much.'

'Rather more than she loved my father, I believe,' he said, his eyes turning to points of green ice. 'It's worth a substantial sum of money.'

Caroline coloured and swallowed hard. She'd opened her mouth, and had managed to put her foot in it.

'In that case I shall guard it with my life,' she said with a grin.

'Has your cat settled in well?' he asked, nodding to Bertram who was busy cleaning his leg on the bed.

'Bertram's a good traveller. He's had some food and water and has made himself right at home.'

'And you? Is the room to your liking?'

'The room has a fantastic view over

the countryside. Would it be possible for me to do some sketching?'

Rafe's smile faded, and Caroline had the distinct impression that she had said the wrong thing. What could possibly be wrong with sketching?

'You're an artist?'

'I'm more of a designer, a craft person, really. Artists do one-offs, but my work is designed to be reproduced hundreds of times. I work in textiles, mainly counted cross-stitch at the moment. Not only do I design charts, but the company I founded also produces mail-order kits and other accessories for people who do needle-work.'

'And is your company successful?'

'Last year we were voted most innovative stitchery company from one of the major cross-stitch magazines and best customer service from yet another. I believe we're one of the fastest growing needlework companies in the world. In fact, I plan to spend part of my holiday going over the latest finance proposals. We have this opportunity to move into Europe in a big way, but it's going to take capital.'

Caroline tried to put the problems with the bank, the overdraft and the tentative refusal of the loan without additional backing out of her mind.

'If you'd like, I'd be happy to take a look at the proposals. I have a few contacts in the City. And if they are up to scratch . . .'

'You don't need to.'

'You're playing my fiancée and helping to save my home. It's the least I can do.'

Rafe took her hand, the hand with the engagement ring, and brought it to his lips. A tremor ran along her arm. Caroline swallowed and withdrew her hand. A giant weight seemed to roll off her back. She'd almost given up hope about the expansion.

'If you're sure, it'd be a big help.'

'I can't promise anything concrete, but if your business is as successful as you say, arranging the finance shouldn't be a problem.'

Caroline examined the wallpaper pattern, trying to concentrate on the loops of flowers, rather than his eyes.

'If your cousins are arriving soon, I'd best change. I doubt your great aunt will appreciate meeting me in my travelling clothes, if she is anything like the way you describe her.'

Rafe seemed lost in thought for a moment.

'Yes, I suppose Aunt Alice will expect my fiancée to be properly dressed,' he said at last.

Caroline nodded.

'It wouldn't do to give the game away quickly. I'd imagine your fiancée wouldn't wear things like this.'

She suddenly had an image of how the perfect girl for him would look, and knew that she couldn't ever look that elegant or polished.

'My fiancée will wear what she wants. There might be times I'd like her not to be properly dressed.'

'However, meeting your aunt would not be one of those times.'

She felt the first flickers of heat on her cheeks, and tried to keep from blushing. Caroline held the door open and pointed.

'If you'll give me a few minutes . . . '

He lifted one eyebrow.

'I look forward to the transformation, with anticipation. When you're ready, I shall be in the drawing-room. It is the second door on the right downstairs.'

Caroline sat down with a thump on the bed. What was she thinking about? She barely knew the man, and his opinion of her appearance was important? It didn't make sense. It was shock, a delayed reaction to waking up to find her flat covered in plaster dust and rubble.

She was not going to be attracted to this man. She was not going to allow herself to care one single bit about what he thought. She was merely going to hold up her end of a bargain.

She tried to think of other things besides the touch of his lips on hers as she changed into something more suitable.

3

'So, sweet coz, where is this fiancée of yours? Has she disappeared off the face of the earth?'

Jenna sat in the chair nearest the fire in the drawing-room, wrapped tightly in a baby pink cashmere shawl. Her stilettos lay abandoned for the moment on the floor. She tapped one of her fingernails against the cup of peppermint tea she cradled. Rafe could smell the heavy, expensive perfume she practically bathed in from where he stood near the door.

'She's getting changed,' Rafe explained for the fifth time. 'I told you she returned from London a few minutes before you arrived.'

Rafe glanced at the door. He tried to make idle chat with his aunt and cousin, but his mind kept returning to Caroline. It had been more than an hour since he'd left her bedroom, and she still hadn't made an appearance. Perhaps he shouldn't have taken a chance on the girl.

'There you are,' he said as Caroline suddenly appeared in the doorway.

Dressed in a black top and cream trousers with large turquoise earrings swinging from her ears, she didn't look nearly as windswept, but he was pleased to see a few tendrils escaping around her forehead.

He'd barely met the woman, and theirs wasn't to be the sort of relationship that had any entanglements, he reminded himself. She was a means to an end, and nothing more.

She hesitated before coming towards him. He went to meet her halfway, intending to kiss her. She turned her head at the last moment and his lips brushed her cheek.

'Well, there's no need to ask who this girl is,' his cousin's husband boomed.

Rafe draped his arm casually around Caroline's waist, holding her a fraction closer to his side than strictly necessary.

'This is Caroline.'

He was unable to resist dropping a kiss on the top of her head for effect.

'Well, thank goodness for that,' Jenna said from her spot by the fire. 'I was beginning to wonder if you were a figment of my cousin's overactive imagination. After all, nobody had met you or knew anything about you, not even your name. It's Caroline, isn't it? You know I'm sure Rafe called you something else when we spoke on the phone a few days ago.'

'I've been very busy, working and moving up here.'

The words tumbled out of Caroline's mouth much too quickly. She paused, took a deep breath and tried again.

'I'm glad we finally have a chance to meet. I've heard so much about you and your husband.'

'All settled in? I was beginning to get concerned,' Rafe said.

'Bertram took longer to settle than I thought, and I needed a shower after what happened earlier,' Caroline answered.

She stopped abruptly, blushing. Jenna looked at her with narrowed eyes. Caroline wanted the floor to open and swallow her. She had to say something, anything. Everyone was looking at her.

'Bertram is my cat. Because I am spending so much time here, I . . . we thought . . . '

'We thought it would be a good idea if Caroline brought her cat up here to live,' Rafe finished smoothly for her. 'The cattery bills were beginning to get expensive, and it made very little sense for Caroline to continue to be based in London, as I have to be up here most of the time. She arrived back from London literally a half hour before you arrived.'

He winked at Caroline, who was now holding out her hand to the older lady, who took it with a twinkling smile.

'I've so looked forward to meeting you, Lady Alice.'

This time none of her words betrayed her nervousness.

'You should do something about your hair.'

There was a faint note of disapproval in Lady Alice's voice.

Caroline blushed and pushed an escaping strand back into place. It had taken her twenty minutes to get the hairstyle right, and within five minutes, her hair was springing about like it had a mind of its own. She wanted to be the picture of elegance she was sure Rafe had painted of his fiancée, but her hair wouldn't co-operate.

'I like it just the way it is,' Rafe said before she had a chance to reply. 'Honestly, Aunt, you'll have Caroline thinking you're a dragon.'

Howard gave a short laugh.

'Before I married Jenna, I used to quake at the mere mention of Lady . . . forgive me . . . Aunt Alice. Now, Ms Adams, what line of business are you in? Rafe said you were an independent business woman.'

'I own a company which designs and manufactures counted stitch kits and accessories. I don't do many sayings, mainly pictures that I then translate into designs on fabric.'

Aunt Alice rapped her stick on the floor.

'Where in London is your company located?'

'In a lovely, old warehouse conversion in Bankside at the moment.'

Caroline tried not to think about the letter she'd received from Howard's company.

'Bankside, eh? I have a project starting there in a few weeks in a rundown, old converted factory. Have to get rid of the tenants first though. Not that they matter very much as some of them are behind on the rent. It's the concept of the thing, wide open space, perfect for a businesswoman such as yourself.'

Howard gave a short laugh that sounded more like a grunt. Caroline longed to ask why he thought so little of the people already there and the change he was making in their lives.

'Caroline has moved up here.'

'What's that, Rafe? Of course, I keep forgetting.'

Howard reached into his pocket and pulled out a business card. He winked at Caroline who automatically took the card, glanced at it and put it down on the mantelpiece.

'Just in case something happens and you change your mind, about maintaining a studio in London, of course.'

Howard smiled ingratiatingly at Rafe who did not return the smile.

'So you're an artistic type,' Lady Alice said. 'Rafe's mother is a painter. She did portraits at one time, but now does something else, abstracts, I think. Painted wonderful portraits, but she didn't have any staying power. Do you have staying power?'

'I'm not sure what you mean, Lady . . . '

The old lady held up a forefinger.

'I mean, Aunt Alice.'

Caroline felt her face grow red.

'Emily loved her husband, of that I'm

45

sure, but she couldn't cope with the rigours of living in a castle and not London. Like a moth, she was attracted to the bright lights and eventually they consumed her.'

'Consumed her?'

'She left her husband and child to pursue her career. Dreadful mess. Nothing and no-one ever satisfies her for long. I suppose it's the artistic temperament or some such nonsense.'

Aunt Alice sniffed.

'Aunt, you talk as if Emily is dead,' Jenna said with some disdain. 'Howard and I went to an exhibition of her paintings only three weeks ago. She was very chatty and clearly pleased to see us. Rafe, your mother doesn't understand why you shut yourself away up here. You should see her more often. She was amazed when I told her that you were getting married. You know, she thought Howard's plan for the castle . . . '

'Jenna!'

There was a warning in Howard's

voice. Jenna put her hand to her lips.

'Silly me, prattling away. Howard has finished his drink by the way.'

Out of the corner of her eye, Caroline could see Rafe's jaw become very set. His hands balled into fists, but the rest of his body was completely still. His green eyes burned with an intense flame that looked about to explode. She had to do something. She walked over and put her arm through his.

'Rafe and his mother aren't very close, but we wanted to tell her in person.'

She was surprised at her capacity to lie with a straight face and steady voice. Normally she blushed or stammered.

'I don't understand one thing. Why should Howard have any plans for this castle? I understood the castle belonged to Rafe.'

'Only if he fulfils all the conditions of his uncle's will. I'm sure Rafe has explained all about that, hasn't he?'

Jenna widened her blue eyes as she spoke and batted them at Rafe with a smirk. Caroline tightened her grip on Rafe's arm.

'Yes, he has. Do you have some problem with the terms?'

Jenna shrugged.

'Not in the slightest. Let's see, how long has Great Uncle Jack been dead? I make it nearly seven years.'

'That's enough, Jenna,' Aunt Alice said, and her voice held an edge of steel. 'We are here to meet Rafe's bride-to-be, not discuss the finer points of my late brother's will.'

Jenna subsided into a sulky silence.

'And what does your family think about you marrying and moving up to Northumberland, Caroline?'

Under Aunt Alice's sharp gaze, Caroline didn't even consider lying.

'They died years ago.'

Instantly the room went quiet and Caroline braced herself for the polite expression of grief and sympathy. But how could they know? How could she begin to explain what it was like to lose all your family in an instant to strangers? She heard the polite murmurings from Aunt Alice.

'How did they die?' Jenna ventured.

'Car crash. A drunk driver jumped a light in a stolen car,' Caroline replied, trying to keep her voice steady.

Caroline felt Rafe's hand on her shoulder.

'Jenna,' he said as he gave the shoulder a squeeze, 'it's not an appropriate topic of conversation. It's something that Caroline still finds very painful. Tonight is for happy thoughts, not sad ones.'

Caroline looked up into his eyes and her heart turned over. He understood — not only understood, but was willing to protect. She swallowed hard. Nobody understood, ever, but he did. She wanted to thank him but the words wouldn't come. He gave her a small nod and removed his hand. Who was this man that he could get under her skin like that? She'd only known him a few short hours. It was the strangeness of the situation, nothing else. Her mind was working overtime, reading things into his words.

'What's for supper, Worthington, old man?'

Howard rubbed his hands together, and looked hopeful.

'I didn't know what time everyone would arrive, so I had Mrs Dodds make a game pie, and leave the potatoes baking in the bottom oven of the Aga.'

'Does she still use her mother's recipe?'

Aunt Alice leaned over towards Caroline and said in a conspiratorial whisper, 'I used to love her mother's game pie so much that as a child I was caught more than once raiding the larder.'

Later, between the game pie, the potatoes and a green salad, Caroline felt full. Normally, she picked at her food, grabbing a sandwich to eat while she worked on her latest design.

The conversation moved from politics to the state of English cricket and back. Mostly she let the conversation wash over her. During one of Howard's long monologues on why the country was going to the dogs, she found her eyes closing. She sat up with a start and tried to concentrate.

Caroline was impressed by how deftly Rafe managed to deflect questions about their supposed relationship. However, once the after-dinner coffee had been poured and they were all seated in the drawing-room, Jenna asked with sugar-coated sweetness and daggered eyes, 'So, when exactly are you two marrying?'

Caroline choked on her coffee. She looked wildly at Rafe for help.

'We haven't set a date yet,' she mumbled into the cup, hoping the explanation would do.

'Why not?'

'We wanted to talk to Aunt Alice in person,' Rafe replied, his face showing no hint of being surprised or upset by the question.

It was only a matter of minutes, seconds maybe, before the whole charade was laid bare before the assembled group. She desperately tried to think of a plausible explanation as to why they'd perpetrated this shabby trick. Her tired mind was not furnishing any explanations.

Once it was revealed, there was no way Aunt Alice would allow Rafe extra time for anything. It was clear from her words before supper that she expected to hear the patter of tiny legitimate Worthington feet. She didn't look like the sort of woman who could forgive a trick easily.

Time, play for time. Come on, you can do this. You can help him think. There has to be a reason.

Her heartbeat raced as her mind groped for the smallest of straws.

'I'm here now.' The lady's voice sounded strong, but there was an unmistakable edge to it. 'What could be a better time to set the date?'

'We're thinking of later in the year,' Caroline said, the words tumbling out before she could stop them.

Caroline wiped her palms on her trousers, and cold sweat trickled down the back of her neck. This was going too far, way too far.

'I've always fancied an autumn wedding. I think the colours of the trees are so lovely in mid-October,' she said.

'I'm not a fan of autumn weddings. Besides, I hate travelling during the winter months.'

'Perhaps next spring then.'

'You know, I have a really wild idea,' Jenna said, opening her eyes wide. 'Why don't you get married while we're here? You can have a large reception later, but a quiet ceremony now, with Aunt Alice. I'm sure she'd love that, wouldn't you, Aunt Alice?'

'I think that is a remarkable idea.' Howard's voice dripped with saccharine charm. 'It'd solve all sorts of problems. Jenna and I could serve as your witnesses.'

Caroline looked at Rafe, uncertain what to do or say. She couldn't plead family concerns. She'd told them that her family was dead. She tried to think, to come up with a plan, any sort of plan. Right now, her mind refused to come up with one solid reason why they shouldn't be married straight away, except the real one. And she couldn't do that to Rafe, not after what had happened earlier. He'd understood. There had been empathy, not false sympathy.

Caroline clenched her jaw. This was a fight, and she wasn't going to blink first. No prisoners. It was her honour at stake. She'd never given into bullies before and she wasn't about to now.

'It may be Aunt Alice's only chance,' Jenna added. 'A special licence wouldn't take too long. What do you say, Rafe, Caroline?'

Rafe looked at Caroline. Tension gripped her body but she wasn't giving in. She was fighting her corner in a way he could never have even hoped for. The way she squashed each of Jenna's points was marvellous. Any second Jenna would explode and all her plans would be laid bare. Could Ms Adams hold out for another moment? He could almost see the steam rising from Jenna's ears.

One little push from him might do the trick.

'It isn't up to me. It's up to Caroline. I think you had your heart set on a church wedding, didn't you, sweetheart?'

Caroline's shoulders stiffened and she gave him a beautiful smile. Jenna's face flushed. Her bottom lip stuck out. It was starting. The temper tantrum was starting.

Together they'd do it. Come on, Caroline, finish her off, he thought.

'Yes, a church wedding with all the trimmings — white dress, pretty flower girls and towering wedding cake. Nothing is planned but it has been a dream of mine since childhood to have a proper white wedding.'

Rafe wanted to punch the air. He wanted to throw his arms around Caroline and spin her round and round. Once again, Ms Adams had made the perfect response. There was a second's pause, two. His breath caught in his throat.

'You could have a blessing in the church at a later date. It's not as if you are big churchgoers, are you? It would mean so much to Aunt Alice.'

Jenna leaned back in her chair, arms crossed, eyes narrowed. Rafe swore under his breath as Jenna neatly closed that avenue. The temper tantrum was so close. He could almost taste victory.

'Rafe, Caroline.' Aunt Alice's voice and eyes held a note of unspeakable longing and desire. 'I know it is a hard thing to ask, but will you marry while I'm here? It would mean so much to me.'

It was over. Rafe saw Caroline hesitate. They'd been close, so close but he couldn't ask her to continue. She'd agreed to the pretend engagement, not a real marriage. His mind groped for the words to signal his surrender. He saw Jenna preen herself. She knew. He cleared his throat.

'Aunt Alice — '

Caroline interrupted, her voice clear and confident and her eyes fixed unwaveringly on Jenna.

'When you put it like that, Aunt Alice, how can we possibly refuse?'

Her first thought in the absolute silence that followed was triumphant. Eat dirt, Jenna.

She barely restrained herself from raising her fists in the air. Her eyes met Rafe's. He gave a thumbs-up and had a big grin on his face. Teamwork. She leaned back in her chair, muscles trembling, exhilaration coursing through her veins, victory!

It wasn't until later, back in the bedroom, when she sat on the bed stroking Bertram that the enormity of what she had said and done began to sink in.

'Oh, help,' she whispered aloud, burying her face in Bertram's fur. 'What did I say? What have I done? What have I done?'

4

As soon as her eyes opened the next morning, Caroline pulled on a pair of grey jogging pants, an over sized T-shirt and her favourite red sweatshirt, before heading out into the woods.

Her mind whirled from last night and her dreams had been filled with images of Rafe. A walk had to be the answer. Had she actually agreed to marry Rafe? What could have possessed her?

Her dating policy was very strict — she didn't unless she knew the man for at least three months. Her parents had been best friends before they married, and they'd had such a happy marriage that Caroline was determined to follow their lead. So far, no-one had matched up to her ideal and she wasn't about to give up her single status for second best.

Caroline gave a small laugh at the

memory of Jenna's jaw-dropping face when she announced this marriage would take place in days. The look on that woman's face had made it worthwhile last night, but today, was this man worth giving up her single status for? Why, oh, why had she agreed? And how was she going to get out of this mess?

In a small clearing, Caroline saw a ring of mushrooms, with a scattering of empty acorn cups, almost like the remains of a party. On impulse she stepped into the ring, closed her eyes tightly and wished.

'Please may I find the right man for me. Please may I find a love like my parents had.'

She opened her eyes, and self-consciously stepped out of the ring. The words had tumbled out from some-where deep inside her, somewhere she had forgotten existed. Until yesterday, she didn't even think she needed a man, and now she was wishing for one.

If she was being honest, she knew

which one she was wishing for, one with deep green eyes, a crooked smile and long, tapered fingers. One, she reminded herself, who was not even remotely interested in her.

She placed her hands on her hips and breathed in deeply, enjoying the smell of the woods. It had to be that — something in the air, not a longing for romance. It was mere whimsy.

A little way beyond the fairy ring, she found a large stone to sit on. The castle, framed by a mixture of interesting trees, gave Caroline an idea. She took out her notebook and quickly started sketching. It was as if the floodgates opened. Barely had she started to sketch her first idea when another came. After months of failure and heartbreak, suddenly the book was taking shape before her eyes.

Caroline paused to rub her stiff shoulder and hand. She glanced back through almost ten pages of drawings. There were a number of good ideas. The rough sketch showing a knight riding to the rescue of a fair maiden had definite possibilities, as did the one where the maiden was embracing the knight after her rescue. She tried to ignore the fact that the knight's face bore more than a passing resemblance to Rafe's.

'Good morning, you're an early riser this morning.'

Caroline jumped at the sound of Rafe's voice, snapping her pencil point. She frowned slightly. She glanced behind her, and could see his lips twitching upwards.

'I didn't think anyone would be up yet. It was so lovely this morning . . . '

'Yes, it is certainly lovely,' he interrupted, his tone low and quiet.

Caroline closed her notebook and looked up at the man. It had been no dream. Even in the early morning, Rafe Worthington was impossibly handsome, and impossibly unavailable, Caroline reminded herself. The woman he eventually settled down with was sure to have a pedigree as long as her arm and know everything there was to know about running an estate and castle instinctively.

'Have you lived at the castle long?' she enquired.

'I've lived here most of my life. My great uncle took me in after . . . well, after my mother left to find herself, and my father died.'

Without waiting for an invitation, Rafe sat down beside her on the rock. He motioned for the collie with him to lie down. Caroline was impressed by the way the dog obeyed his master instantly.

'Were you being groomed to run the estate?'

'No. I never thought that I would,' Rafe said after a long pause. 'I loved the land. It seemed like Uncle Jack would go on for ever. When my great uncle became too ill to look after the estate properly, luckily my own business was such that I was able to move here and help.'

'Were you involved in estate management then?'

Rafe laughed, a short, bitter laugh.

'My great uncle wouldn't let me. He insisted I learn something other than farming, as it was doubtful that the land could ever pay. He didn't want me wasting my life on an old man's dream.'

'And you became?'

'A barrister. My great uncle loved the law nearly as much as he loved the land. He thought it would be a suitable profession.'

'Do you still practise? How do you find the time to run the estate and be a barrister?' Caroline asked.

'When he died nearly seven years ago, my uncle left me most of the estate. It was typical of the man.'

He stared off in the distance for a few minutes before continuing.

'He never told me. It was only when the will was read that I learned he had entrusted me with it. My uncle still believed in dreams. He reckoned that I was the person most likely to keep it safe for the next generation. It is large enough to give me a decent living, and I don't miss the Bar or the law.'

'I'm sorry. You must miss him.'

Her face burned. She'd pried too close. She braced herself for the inevitable rebuff. Rafe was silent for a moment before answering.

'My uncle and I were great friends. Down the years, he was my rock. He was always there for me. He taught me everything I know about farming and managing an estate. But he had a good innings. He was eighty-five when he died.'

'It doesn't matter how old people are when they die, the loss is still there.'

Rafe gave her hand a squeeze.

'Are you going to show me what you have been sketching so industriously this morning?' he teased as he reached for the notebook.

'I thought you must have seen enough of my work last night to last a lifetime,' Caroline responded lightly, moving the notebook over to her other side. 'Your aunt spent an hour going over the sketches.'

'You're a talented artist.' He laughed at Caroline's expression. 'I mean craftperson. It's fantastic what you can create out of a few pencil strokes. I'd never realised how much went into designing needlework until I listened to you and Aunt Alice talk.'

'Hopefully you weren't as bored as Jenna and Howard seemed to be.'

'Jenna is bored by anything that does not involve the worship of her.' He reached for the notebook. 'Your sketches, if you please, milady?'

Caroline held the notebook as far away from him as she could. He mustn't see that knight, anything but the knight.

'I . . . I really do not like showing anyone my rough sketches.'

'I'm hardly just anyone, Caroline. I'm your fiancé. That gives me certain rights.'

His eyes were dancing and there was a faint upward curve to his lips.

'Only until Jenna loses her temper.'

'I wanted to thank you for what you

said last night. I didn't expect that. Hopefully, you won't have to go through with your promise. However, come the wedding day, I won't hold you to it, if you decide to back out.'

'I don't see how I can back out now, not without upsetting your aunt, and making matters much worse. No, I meant what I said. I will marry you, if it comes to it. Besides, it's going to be in name only, and then a divorce after a suitable interval.'

Caroline wondered whom she was trying to convince.

'You don't know what a debt I owe you.'

'I'm doing it for the pleasure of spiting Howard Steel. People like that get me angry.'

The excuse sounded so feeble. She couldn't tell him the truth, not and maintain her self-respect. How to explain being encased in ice for ten years and suddenly feeling you made contact with someone, a connection — it was exhilarating and frightening at the same time.

'You don't just change your life like that to spite someone.'

'Well, there is your offer to help out with securing the finance for my company.'

'You mean you'd like some money.'

There was a distinct edge to his voice, hard and cold.

'No, not money.'

Caroline's chin went up. How dare he accuse her of wanting a payoff! She struggled to explain something that would be logical.

'I stand on my own two feet, but it did occur to me that being your wife might open a few doors, might make a few people look favourably on the application. Implications of silent backing, that sort of thing. It's not that Adams' Stitchery needs the money. We need to appear to be on a sound financial footing. Being your wife will do that, just to get my foot in the door.'

'If you say so. Whatever the motive, you have my gratitude.'

She looked up at him and her breath

caught in her throat.

'What will you give me, if I don't take a peek?'

Rafe made a sudden grab and prised the notebook out of her hand. She made a wild grab for it, missed and ended up lying across his lap.

'Anything, anything. Just don't look.'

'Anything?'

His tone made her raise her eyes and look into his face. Immediately she dropped her eyes. She was very aware of where she was, half on and half off his lap. Her tongue licked her bottom lip.

'Almost anything.'

Rafe tilted her chin back with his long forefinger. Slowly, deliberately, he captured her lips with his. She resisted the temptation to immediately give in to the kiss and tried to remind herself of all the reasons why she must not become emotionally involved with this man, reasons that became less and less clear the longer his lips touched hers.

Caroline brought her arms around

Rafe's neck as he clasped her tighter to his chest. She touched his hair with her hand, running her fingers through the curls, not thinking, only feeling.

The sudden sound of a wood pigeon taking off brought Caroline to her senses. What was she doing? What had she been thinking? She broke off the kiss, and stood up, brushing the dirt off her jeans as she did so. For a few seconds they looked at each other, breathing hard. Rafe stood up.

'We seem to be getting a lot of practice in,' he remarked casually.

Caroline straightened her sweatshirt.

'It's getting to be a smooth performance,' she agreed but longed for him to contradict her.

'Quite a polished performance.'

They stared at each other for a heartbeat and then Caroline looked away until she felt able to take the intensity of his eyes.

'That's my sketching done for the morning,' she said briskly changing the subject as she glanced at her watch.

'Hopefully, I haven't missed breakfast.'

Rafe stared at Caroline. What had just happened? He couldn't be attracted to this woman. There were too many echoes of his parents' relationship, and yet, it was all he could do to keep from pulling her into his arms again.

'I'm confident we can find something. Did you let anyone know that you were out here?' he asked.

Caroline bent down and picked up a coloured pencil she'd dropped as she began to pack away her supplies.

'No, I didn't see anyone. Should I have?'

'This isn't London, Caroline. Things happen. The weather changes, you get stuck in boggy ground, you get lost. A thousand things could happen. The fells are not necessarily safe.'

He tried to remind himself of all the reasons why he wasn't going to get involved with some city girl, some girl who would turn out to be like his mother — selfish, self-absorbed, self-indulgent and supremely vain.

'I can take care of myself.' Caroline put her hands on her hips. 'And the castle is clearly visible from here.'

'You may think you're safe, but what if you weren't? It's a big area. Where would the men begin to look? If Fly and I hadn't seen your red shirt on our way back from the farm, somebody might have raised an alarm, all for nothing.'

He knew he was making excuses, to her, to himself, giving a reason for stopping. It was nothing to do with the fact he couldn't get her out of his mind, nothing to do with wanting to spend time with her.

'I can take care of myself,' Caroline repeated. 'I've been doing a pretty good job of it for the last twenty-seven years.'

'Stubborn, that's what she is, stubborn, Fly,' Rafe said to his dog. 'The house rules are you tell someone or you leave a note. It's called politeness. Shall we have breakfast?'

Caroline hesitated as Rafe strode off with his collie at his heels, very much the lord of the castle. She knew he was right, but it didn't make it any easier. She ran after him. He stopped and waited for her, smiling.

'I'm glad you decided to see reason.'

'My stomach heard the word breakfast. Besides, you have my notebook.' She held out her hand. 'If you please?'

'I don't believe you've given me anything for its ransom.'

'A kiss. I gave you a kiss.'

Caroline felt her face flame as she remembered the intensity of the kiss they'd shared.

'But did I ask for it? Your kiss was given freely and your response delightful.' Rafe's eyes sparkled and Caroline shook her head in confusion.

If he saw the sketches — no, he couldn't see the sketches. It would give everything away. They were sketches, just sketches, but what if he drew the wrong conclusion?

'But I thought . . . ' She paused and tried again. 'That is, you're not going to look at it, are you? My notebook is very private.'

'You intrigue me. With each word, you make the temptation greater, but am I a gentleman or not?'

'A gentleman, definitely a gentleman.'

'Hmm, I'll consider the request, since you beg so nicely.'

'You can keep it.'

Rafe threw back his head and laughed.

'If it means so much to you.'

He held it out and Caroline nearly snatched it from his hand.

'But I will claim my payment, later.'

'Is that a threat or a promise?'

Rafe put his arm around her shoulders and pulled her closer.

'You decide.'

5

Rafe glanced at the woman beside him, matching him stride for stride as they neared the forecourt of the castle. Impulsive, she was, beautiful, generous. How could he best describe her? The more he saw, the more he wanted to see, but Ms Adams would leave soon. Rafe clenched his jaw. She was on holiday and holiday romances, like his parents', led to disaster.

He took his arm from her shoulders, and quickened his pace.

'I trust you can find your way to the castle now.'

'I always could. I may live in London, but I'm not a total ignoramus.'

'Good, you've relieved my mind. I'm confident, you'll remember the house rules now, even for a short walk. It saves time in the long run.'

The words came out harsher than

Rafe intended. Caroline's face fell.

'Now that I know, I won't forget.'

Rafe forced his hands not to reach out to her, to smooth that one strand of hair back from her forehead. He'd no doubt that his parents' relationship had started in the same manner.

His mother had been on holiday from London, a young artist in the first flush of success, and his father was finding his feet as Uncle Jack's estate manager. It was sudden and swift, and over just as quickly, with disastrous consequences for his father who never recovered from his wife leaving him with a two-year-old toddler to look after.

Within the year, he was dead — a shooting accident, or so they said, but Rafe knew different. The whispers that silenced as he walked past told him, as did his Uncle Jack after he'd had too much to drink and warned him against flighty women. The schoolboys in the dorm whispering in the dark after lights out were the worst.

Rafe turned away from Caroline. He refused to make the same mistake. The only thing that was important was the castle, and she was the means of securing its ownership, nothing more. He pushed the thought of her softly-yielding lips and the taste of her sun-warmed skin from his mind.

'You can look after yourself for the rest of the day?'

'It's not like I was expecting to be entertained,' she said.

'Well, well, it's the two lovebirds. Not having a quarrel I hope.' Jenna's voice rang out from the doorway.

'What are you talking about, Jenna?' Rafe asked.

The woman shrugged.

'I thought for a second I heard raised voices. I wanted to find sweet Caroline and discover if she has a wedding outfit.'

'The whole wedding is very sudden, Jenna. You can't expect her to have chosen her outfit already.'

'Caroline can speak for herself, can't you, dear?'

Rafe's hand balled into a fist at that false tone and smug smile of Jenna's, the one she always used to twist people around her little finger.

'I have a voice, but no outfit,' Caroline stated firmly.

'I had the most marvellous idea. It came to me this morning in bed. We can go shopping. My friend told me about this marvellous little shop in Corbridge. I thought we might get a bite to eat for lunch, make it a real girl's day out. Unless you have other plans, of course.'

Caroline made a noise, but Rafe cut her off.

'I'm sorry, Jenna, but Caroline and I both need to go into Hexham to the Register Office. We need to get a licence, and if we don't do it today before one o'clock, we'll have to wait until after the weekend to get the licence. No licence, no wedding.'

'What do you mean, surely you have a licence?'

'Why should we? We only set the date

last night,' Caroline replied as she batted her eyelashes.

'But it takes sixteen days for a licence to become valid. Surely you can't expect us to wait around for that period of time.'

'And why not?' Caroline retorted.

'Of course, you won't have to wait for sixteen days.'

Rafe put his arm around Caroline, drawing her close.

'We're paying extra and getting married by special licence. We only need one clear day between application and marriage. Today's Friday, so we should be able to marry on Monday.'

Caroline stiffened in his arms, but remained there as Jenna's eyes darted from Rafe to herself. She opened her mouth as if to scream, but pressed her lips together to form a narrow band of dark red.

'You know this has given me the most marvellous idea.'

'Does she ever have an idea that isn't marvellous?' Caroline whispered in Rafe's ear.

'And your idea is?'

'Why don't we throw a party in honour of your marriage? When was the last time you gave a party, Rafe? Probably years and years ago. It doesn't have to be a large party, fifty or so. You go get the licence and I'll organise the party. Howard says I'm truly a marvel at such things. Unless . . . '

'Unless what?'

'Unless there is some reason why you don't want to introduce your bride to your friends.'

'I never said that.'

Rafe ran his free hand through his hair. His friends Caroline might enjoy but the bunch of hyenas Jenna would invite was quite another thing!

'We'd hoped for a quiet wedding, Jenna. Rafe and I are not party people.' Caroline's voice was firm.

'But the bride of Haydon Castle must be introduced to the county set. It'll be a chance for Aunt Alice to see her old friends. We can have a buffet supper or maybe only drinks and nibbles.'

Jenna clapped her hands, but she looked at Rafe with an intense look.

'As I said before, what are you trying to hide?'

'We're not trying to hide anything,' Caroline said in a low but confident voice. 'In my opinion, the party is unnecessary.'

'Which is precisely the reason why I want to organise this party for you. One thing less for you to worry about.'

Rafe sighed.

'If you are so insistent, you can make out a plan but I want to see a full plan before you start telephoning caterers or inviting guests.'

'What do you think she is up to?' Caroline asked in a low voice as Jenna retreated swiftly into the castle.

'I don't know, but I doubt she is planning this party for our benefit. However, it will keep her out of mischief for the time being.' He pulled Caroline closer. 'You needn't worry, there won't be a party.'

Caroline took his arm from her waist.

'I wasn't worried. I figured that one out all by myself.'

* * *

Caroline was pleased she'd left her jumper behind when she finished climbing the hill from the carpark to the square in front of the abbey in Hexham. Rafe led the way down a narrow lane and across an immaculate green lawn to the register's office.

Rafe put his hand on her back. The warmth from it spread throughout her body. Although she knew the simple touch meant nothing to him, it gave her the courage to go on. It had been her suggestion after all. There was no way she was going to allow Jenna to triumph.

The whole process took no more than a few minutes, and then they were back out in the warm June sunshine. Everything about the scene was the same as a few minutes ago — white clouds, blue sky, green grass, but somehow it was different. It was no longer a game or a bad joke — she was committed.

She looked at the man who she would marry in three days, the man she hadn't known existed yesterday. A lump grew in her throat.

'Are you OK? You look like you could do with a cup of coffee, or maybe something stronger,' Rafe said.

She smiled but felt the tears pooling in her eyes, threatening to spill down her cheeks. She blinked rapidly.

'I think I got up earlier than I realised.'

'Coffee it is. There's a little coffee shop around to the right.'

Rafe touched her elbow and guided her into the nearby coffee shop. Caroline tried to ignore the butterflies in her stomach. She tried to concentrate on other things besides how strong and capable his hand felt.

'Northumberland is a much prettier

place than I thought it would be. England how it should be, with plenty of green fields, old buildings and old-fashioned coffee shops. Not the quick-pace lifestyle of London with high rises, fast food and even faster people.'

'I'm pleased you are enjoying your holiday. There's so much to see in Northumberland. Perhaps after this little difficulty of mine is solved . . . '

Rafe's eyes were dark, unfathomable pools of green. Her breath caught. She was reading into the statement what she wanted to hear. He was being polite, and she thought he wanted to spend time with her. She needed to take a grip on her emotions, now, before it was too late.

Rafe raised his mug to hers, clinking them softly together.

'To us, and to our marriage.'

Caroline peeped at him over the rim of her coffee cup. Retreat, she ordered herself. Build a wall. Think distance.

'You mean to the defeat of Jenna and Howard.'

'That's exactly what I mean. You said

it much better than I could.'

The smile didn't quite reach Rafe's eyes.

'I think Hexham is beautiful. If we have time, I'd like to make a few quick sketches,' she said quickly to fill the void of silence.

Rafe looked at his watch and Caroline was reminded again that she wasn't that important in his life.

'I have to get back. There's a pile of paperwork I have to finish, and then I need to check the men.'

She tried to swallow her disappointment. Somehow, she'd hoped he wanted to spend some time with her, get to know her better.

'It's OK. It was just a thought. There is plenty to do at the castle. I need to see how Bertram is getting on.'

'If you finish your coffee quickly, maybe I can spare a few minutes.'

'No, it's fine. There are plenty of places to sketch around the castle.'

She took a large gulp of coffee, and wiped her hand across her lips.

'That's all I need. Fully recovered,

and ready to go. It is amazing how much a cup of coffee can do for you. I only need to get a new mobile now. Just into my holiday and I'm already getting withdrawal symptoms.'

'If you need to use the internet, let me know. We have all facilities.'

'I'll do that.'

After a short stroll, Caroline made her phone purchase.

'I've got the phone,' she said as she rejoined Rafe at the shop door. 'I think it's about time we returned to the castle. I need to know what has been happening at the studio and I've wasted enough of your time.'

The afternoon light was fading fast as Caroline drew a few more lines on the second draft of her knight picture. She had the composition almost right, the knight on his horse looking down at the lady as she offered him roses, with the castle in the background, but the roses needed to be moved upwards and the lady's face turned more towards the viewer.

'Even condemned prisoners get to

take their turn around the courtyard,' Rafe's voice broke into her thoughts.

Caroline jumped slightly at the sound of his voice.

'I have been up here a while,' she said. 'It is the perfect place to draw. Did you paint those canvases, by the way?'

Caroline pointed to a dusty stack of oil paintings.

Rafe crossed the room, and looked through them. Long-buried memories about his mother assaulted him. Some were happy, but most were of when she had gone, and he was trying to hold on to her image, her presence, and pretend she cared about him more than her work and her men.

'My mother's,' he replied.

'Was this her studio?'

'For the short time she was here. Then afterwards when she used to remember she had a son and come to visit.'

'Were you young when your mother left?' Caroline asked softly.

'About two. She wasn't into motherhood. Her career was the most important thing to her.'

'And your father, how old were you when he died?'

'He had a shooting accident shortly afterwards.'

'What a tragedy.'

Caroline could hear the pain in his voice. She wanted to go to him, to comfort him, but stopped in mid-movement. What could she say that hadn't been said a hundred times before? She hated it when people expressed their sympathy for the death of her family, strangers who didn't even know them and couldn't guess how her world had turned upside down.

'It was many years ago. Uncle Jack proved to be a great substitute father, and my mother showed up every now and again when she was between men and needed money and attention. Luckily, Uncle Jack never let her take me away with her. Her enthusiasm for motherhood only ever lasted a few weeks at most.'

'You know this room is one of the

best studios I've ever worked in.'

Caroline tried to change the subject. She had to keep her distance, be unemotional, uninvolved. They'd part soon enough.

'It has brilliant light.'

'I'm pleased you like it. Consider it yours for as long as you are here. After all this work, surely I can tempt you with a scone or two. Mrs Dodds makes some of the world's best scones.'

She quickly gathered her pencils, and placed a cloth over the picture.

'Superstition. I don't like my pictures seen until they are ready.'

Rafe nodded.

'The light's fading so you won't be able to get much more work done today. Perhaps you will join me in a game of chess after tea.'

Caroline looked at the ring on her finger and swallowed hard. She ought to make an appearance, but she had refused to play chess since her family died. Even the thought sent searing pain through her.

'I used to play quite a bit as a girl,' Caroline began, wondering how she could explain.

'Chess is one of those things you never forget.'

Caroline closed her eyes briefly, pushing away the pain. She glanced at Rafe, standing there, so vital, so alive and knew she would accept any excuse to spend more time with him.

'You'll have to be patient.'

'Chess is all about patience. You will find that I'm a very patient man.'

He made a serious face, but the corners of his mouth twitched.

'Then I will take up the offer.'

'You have a bit of dust on your nose.'

Immediately, her hand went to rub it off.

'You're making it worse. Allow me.' He came over, and rubbed her nose lightly with his handkerchief. 'All better.'

He was so close that their bodies nearly touched. She curled her hand, trying not to touch him, but longing for his touch. She tried to remember that this was an in-name-only relationship, that she didn't do casual, but her body seemed to have forgotten that little rule.

Slowly, his hands grasped her elbows and pulled her closer. His lips brushed hers. With a great effort, she turned her head and broke off the kiss.

'The tea will be getting cold,' she said, her voice shaking slightly.

'The tea? Of course, the tea, and afterwards, perhaps we ought to play for more than the mere pleasure of winning.'

She took a step back and tried to control her breathing.

'I thought we agreed that this was to be a purely platonic relationship, that any kissing was to be for the benefit of Jenna or Aunt Alice.'

He raised an eyebrow.

'And what do you call what just happened?'

'A mistake, not to be repeated,' Caroline stated and headed downstairs.

6

The tea was one of those teas that you read about in books but rarely experience, Caroline thought. Its very grandeur intimidated, shouting he, this man whose lips had brushed hers minutes before, inhabits a different world, a world of wealth, prestige and privilege, not her world.

'This is only a small snack, a prelude to supper.'

Howard, his plate groaning with several sandwiches, date bread and both types of cake, with crumbs scattered down his front, gestured to the table.

'It reminds me of the teas we used to have when I was a girl,' Aunt Alice said, accepting a cup of tea from Rafe. 'I do believe Mrs Dodds has used my great-grandmother's china. I used to be terrified of dropping something.'

Caroline felt Rafe's hand on her shoulder. Instinctively she reached out and touched it. The hand was instantly withdrawn. She looked into his face.

'You said scones. This is a feast.'

'Mrs Dodds wanted to do something special.'

'That reminds me, Rafe.' Jenna's voice was shrill and demanding. 'I've done some work on this party. Now what I was thinking is that we should figure on catering for at least one hundred.'

Caroline looked at Jenna, unable to disguise the horror she was feeling. She doubted she could cope socialising with dozens of the great and the good. It was hard enough being here with only Jenna, Howard and Aunt Alice to contend with, pretending she was the beloved fiancée of the master of this castle, when all she was was a nobody, someone who happened to be in a certain place at a certain time when anybody would have done.

'Jenna, I've been thinking as well,'

Rafe was saying. 'I can't afford to take the time. Haymaking will be here in a few short weeks. I'm going to be working all the hours of the day and night, in order to stay on top of things. Any party will have to wait.'

Caroline closed her eyes, relief washing over her. Rafe had said he would take care of her, that he wouldn't let her down. An icy finger of doubt crept in. He wouldn't want to be parading her as his wife in front of his friends. He probably thought she was just fling material. She tightened her jaw and squared her shoulders. The fling wasn't even going to start.

Her stomach somersaulted. She wanted to be more than a bit of fluff. She wanted Rafe Worthington to be more than what he was, than what he was prepared to give. He'd never asked for this, this schoolgirl-like crush.

She tightened her fingers around the teacup. She had to keep a tight control on her emotions.

'Caroline, did you grow up in London?'

Aunt Alice's voice brought her back to the present.

'No, I grew up in Cambridge. My father was a porter at the colleges.'

'Then what made you choose London? Surely you could have set up your studio anywhere. Wouldn't it have made more sense to be closer to your family?'

'Aunt Alice,' Howard cut in before Caroline had a chance to answer, 'there are sound business reasons why Caroline set up in London. She strikes me as a very astute businesswoman.'

Caroline tilted her head.

'I chose London because that is where I went to art college and it is also where I got my first job. I used to find lots of inspiration in the Victoria and Albert Museum, but lately it seems I'm finding more inspiration here with the wide, open skies and the green fields.'

'This is the first time you've lived in the country then?' Aunt Alice asked and

94

Caroline nodded.

'Will wonders never cease?' Jenna said as she poured another cup of tea. 'Rafe, this must be true love. I thought you always swore that you'd only marry a true country girl, brought up in country ways. Tell us please, how did you two meet?'

The silence seemed to stretch a lifetime.

'It must be quite a story. Look, Caroline's face is turning red,' Howard called out.

Caroline refused to look at Rafe.

'We met on holiday,' she said slowly. 'I came up here on holiday. There was a problem with the cottage I rented, and Rafe solved it. There's nothing mysterious about that.'

She was rewarded with a dazzling smile from Rafe.

'Yes, it was a case of love at first sight. Although Caroline was pretty grubby at the time, I was able to spot the potential underneath.'

Caroline felt a warm glow envelop

her. Love at first sight. How her heart wanted those words to be true, but her head knew them for the lie they were. She forced herself to laugh.

'And there you have it, nothing special,' she said.

Jenna's eyes narrowed. Her gaze flicked from Caroline to Rafe.

'There must have been something special to get my cousin to propose. I've lost track of the women in his life who thought they had him.'

'Have you tried any of the scones, Aunt Alice?' Rafe offered the plate. 'Mrs Dodds told me that she made them especially the way you like them.'

Caroline tried to concentrate on sipping her tea and ignore the sinking feeling in the pit of her stomach. She didn't want to think about Rafe and other women. She refused to think about what happened before or what would surely happen after she had returned to her normal life.

Rafe produced a chessboard with its carved chess pieces.

'My great uncle acquired this in Hong Kong in the late Fifties,' he explained, setting up the pieces. 'Caroline promised me a game earlier.'

Chess! Caroline's stomach dropped. What had she been thinking of when she agreed to play? It had taken her years to be able to look at a chessboard without tears falling.

The last thing her father had said to her was, 'Be sure to set up the board and we'll have a game when I get back. I'm just driving your mum and sisters down to the supermarket. It won't take long.'

The board had then stood untouched for three days while he lay in intensive care. The nurses and doctors said her mother and sisters had been killed outright, but her father lingered, more dead than alive. When he breathed his last, she burned the board and the pieces.

Caroline leaned back now in the chair and tried to blot out the memory.

'Are you all right, Caroline? We don't

have to play. It was just a suggestion,' Rafe asked.

'No, I want to play.'

Caroline was surprised, knowing she told the truth. She did want to play, now that the pieces were in front of her and Rafe sat across from her. She watched intently as his hand moved his first piece.

It took a few moves for Caroline to recall the game but once she had countered one of Rafe's moves by moving her knight, all the memories came flooding back. They weren't nearly as bad as she feared. After five moves, she had trouble remembering why she had denied herself the pleasure of playing for so long.

'Are you sure you're OK?' Rafe's soft eyes met hers and his hand covered hers. 'You seemed to have a bad moment.'

'I'm enjoying playing. I'd forgotten how much I like to play.'

She allowed her hand to linger a few seconds longer in his, before she withdrew it to make her next move.

'Hey, I thought you hadn't played for years,' Rafe commented as Caroline captured one of his bishops.

She laughed.

'It's something you never forget, I believe someone who shall remain nameless said so not very long ago.'

'Ah, but I didn't think you'd remember so well.'

Caroline then captured his rook.

'I believe it is checkmate.'

She leaned back in her chair and watched his face as it dropped in disbelief. She could see him going over the moves mentally.

'What exactly were we playing for?' he asked, his eyes intense.

'Nothing in particular.'

Her voice was barely above a whisper as she ignored the butterflies dancing in her stomach. Rafe mouthed back, 'Coward,' and started to set up the game again.

Jenna clapped her hands.

'I've had the most wonderful idea.

Now Rafe and Caroline, I know you
don't want a fuss made of your
wedding, but you will love this surprise.'

'Jenna . . . ' Rafe's voice held a
warning note.

'I want it to be a surprise.'

She blew a kiss and hurried out of
the room.

The next morning, Caroline's head
pounded. She and Jenna had spent the
better part of the morning supposedly
in search of her wedding dress, but in
reality, it was obvious Jenna wanted to
shop for herself.

When Caroline finally found the
perfect dress — a simple white sheath,
costing her her clothes budget for the
next six months — she was past caring
about costs, or budgets, or even how
often she'd wear the dress. She only
knew that the dress fitted in all the right
places.

She wasn't buying the dress because
a certain pair of green eyes would light
up when they saw her in it, she told

herself. She was buying it because, well, you never knew when a dress like that might come in handy. It was an investment! When Jenna suggested trying another shop, Caroline held up the bag.

'I've bought the dress. Now I'd like to get back to the castle to do some sketching outside while the morning light is still good.'

'Spoilsport. You do have time for a coffee, don't you?'

As it was not quite lunchtime, the restaurant they went to was practically empty. Caroline was halfway through her coffee when Jenna suddenly sighed and pushed away her glass of water.

'It's no good, Caroline. I've wrestled with my conscience over this and I have to talk to you about something.'

Caroline felt a breath catch in her throat.

'Is there some problem, something I should know about?'

'Unfortunately, yes.' Jenna looked terribly sad and concerned. 'Caroline, I have to tell you this. You're such a nice person and I feel we are sisters under the skin. I know it will be painful for you, but I have to tell you that Rafe doesn't love you.'

Caroline bit her lip and tried to keep a straight face.

'Don't be silly, Jenna. Rafe and I are getting married.'

Jenna looked slightly put out. She frowned, and then rubbed her thumb and forefinger across her forehead, obviously remembering that frowning caused wrinkles. She tried again.

'I know you're getting married, but I wanted to tell you that Rafe's heart belongs to another.'

The sudden stab of hurt Jenna's words caused surprised Caroline. Where had that come from? It didn't matter whom Rafe's heart belonged to. It couldn't matter. She wouldn't let it matter. She knew it didn't belong to her.

She took a deep breath, and tried not to let Jenna see her words had found their mark.

'I don't know what you are talking about.'

'Howard and I believe that he was planning on marrying someone else, someone called Lisa.'

'He's marrying me, Jenna. We've been engaged for months now.'

'Dear, hasn't he told you about our uncle's will? The only reason he is marrying you is to fulfil his obligations and inherit the castle. It isn't as if he loves you. I feel certain that he loves this other woman. There, I've said it. I had to say it. Don't hate me for it. I didn't want you to make a horrible mistake. You're far too nice a person.'

Caroline narrowed her eyes, and looked at the woman sitting across from her. Jenna's eyes gleamed with barely-concealed triumph.

'Thank you for being so concerned about me, Jenna. I will certainly let Rafe know about the issues you raise.'

Jenna whitened.

'You mustn't do that. He'd only deny it, but search your heart of hearts, and ask yourself, do you really see yourself as mistress of Haydon Castle? Can you cope living with a man you know must despise you?'

Caroline pushed her chair back and stood up.

'I believe, Jenna, you have over-stepped the mark. I think it is best if we pay the bill and go.'

'But you will think on what I've said. After all, I wouldn't want you to make the same mistakes I did the first two times around.'

'Don't worry. I'm not planning on it.'

Her body shook with rage as she walked out of the restaurant.

★   ★   ★

Rafe checked the gravel drive from his study window for the tenth time that morning. So strong was his desire to see Caroline that he then walked through the woods to the spot where she'd sketched yesterday morning. He held his breath as the rock where she had sat came into view, but only a footprint in the mud next to it showed that anyone had ever been there.

Back in the breakfast room, he'd casually questioned Aunt Alice if she knew of Caroline's plans for the morning. She seemed amused at his discomfort when she told him of the shopping trip.

That had been at ten and it was now half-past twelve. There was a pile of papers to be dealt with, but he found himself unable to concentrate. His thoughts kept returning to Caroline and what she was doing. Was there anything, anything at all Jenna could do to poison Caroline against him? It was the castle he wanted to save, he kept telling himself, and Caroline wasn't important.

His blood ran cold. He'd stopped thinking of her as Ms Adams. She was Caroline. This was not going to start. He was not going to follow in his father's footsteps and fall for someone he barely knew.

He let out a sigh of relief when he heard the crunch of the gravel on the drive and the sound of a car door slamming. Fly gave him a funny look from the carpet where he lay, as Rafe went hurrying to the study door. He reached the entrance hall at the same moment as Caroline pulled open the door. She walked in with long, angry strides, glancing neither right nor left. Jenna followed, angry-eyed, but with a triumphant smile on her face.

'Caroline,' he called, 'is everything all right?'

She covered the distance between them in two strides and kissed him with a fierce, angry kiss. He pulled her close.

'That's what I call a hello,' he said, looking down into her eyes.

She smiled back at him, bringing her hand up to his cheek. Rafe could see Jenna's smile had faltered.

'I've been shopping.' Caroline's voice seemed to catch in her throat.

'Do I get to see what you've bought?'

'Honestly, you'd think you people

had not seen each other for weeks, instead of a few short hours,' Jenna said sharply.

Caroline took a step back and Rafe released her instantly.

'We're getting married, Jenna,' she replied quietly.

'So you keep telling me.'

Rafe cocked his head. He'd half hoped Caroline's greeting was genuine, not a stage-managed act for Jenna. He should have known better. Ms Adams was a consummate actress, like his mother.

'Is there something I should know?' he asked Jenna.

'Girl talk, cousin, just girl talk, the sort of thing that bores you silly two seconds after you hear it, but keeps us girls amused.'

Rafe waited until Jenna had left the hall.

'I was wondering if you wanted to go for a walk this afternoon,' he said, with a sudden desire to keep Caroline with him. 'I need to inspect one of the dry stone walls. One of my men reported some stones had been pulled away, and I could do with some company. But if you have to work . . .'

'I'm supposed to be on holiday, remember? I wasn't sure why you were asking me, that's all.'

'What do you mean by that?'

'Nothing, nothing at all.' She paused and continued with a sigh. 'In fact, it's Jenna. I let her get to me during the shopping trip. Did you know she knew about your old fiancée, the one who dumped you?'

'I should have guessed.'

'I kept quiet.'

He strained to hear her whisper, then unable to stop himself, he reached out and touched her velvety soft cheek.

'Once again, I don't know how to thank you.'

She shrugged.

'I told you I'd play my part, and so I shall, but in return I want some honesty from you. I need to know I'm not here to play some sort of silly game, because you and your former fiancée had some fight.'

'I told you the truth, and the reasons why I need a fiancée, a wife. Having met Jenna, can you understand why?'

She gave a soft laugh that made his heart turn over.

'Having met Jenna and Howard, I understand completely. They need to be thwarted at their game.'

'Look, get changed, and we can talk as we walk. A good, brisk walk does wonders for improving moods,' Rafe said quickly before he gave in to the temptation to taste her lips again.

She gave a sideways glance as if she had expected something more.

'If you give me a few minutes, I suspect you're right. The planning is best done where we can't be overheard. The sooner everything is solved, the sooner I can get back to normal.'

7

Caroline tried to concentrate on where she was putting her feet, and not on the man walking next to her. His rebuke about being a city girl two mornings ago still stung. She wanted to prove her boots were more than fashion items.

'Do you need a hand?' Rafe asked as he waited by a stile.

The touch of his hand as he helped her sent shivers down her spine. They locked gazes until she let go of his hand, looked away and started walking quickly across the field.

Caroline kept her eyes on the horizon. She hadn't kept her heart safe for all these years merely to throw it away on some holiday romance. She had her pride, after all. Her mind was in charge, not her body.

It was a physical thing, that was all. The kiss this morning had been for

Jenna's benefit, to show her that her hateful words were wrong, not because she wanted to feel the touch of his lips.

The sound of a stick hitting the ground made her turn around. She watched as Rafe threw the stick for Fly to fetch again. This time the dog caught it in mid-air, before returning to his master's side. Rafe held the stick out to Caroline.

'Why don't you throw the stick for Fly?'

'Could I? Do you think he'd play the game with me? We had a dog when I was growing up, but . . .'

'Fly loves to play fetch. If I had the time, I'd train him to do agility, but I reckon he gets enough exercise as it is.'

He reached down and patted the dog's head. Fly looked pointedly at the stick. Caroline threw it as hard as she could. The dog caught it, and looked between the two people with his head cocked to one side

'Take it to Caroline.' Rafe laughed. 'If

you throw it again, Fly will be your friend for life.'

Caroline refused to examine the remark or the way it made her heart beat faster.

'Somehow, I think I'll tire of this game before you, Fly,' she said, throwing the stick for a third time.

'You might be right on that one.'

Rafe whistled to Fly and started off across the field with the dog at his heels. Up here on the fells, it was easy to forget there was another world beyond green fields, stone walls and the clear blue sky.

She stood for a moment, watching the man and his dog striding towards the next stile. Then, breaking into a run, she caught up with them. Their arms nearly touching, she matched him stride for stride.

When Caroline stopped to re-tie her boot, she glanced at her watch. They'd been walking for about an hour. A strange, low moaning noise filled the air. Something or someone was in pain.

'Rafe,' she called, 'what's that noise?'

Rafe was a little way ahead with Fly by his side. The dog's head was cocked to one side. He listened intently for a few seconds. On the other side of the wall, they found a group of seven sheep stuck in a bog, bleating frantically. One lay half buried in the mud and the others were very distressed. With one leap, Fly cleared the wall, Rafe not far behind. Caroline ran up to the wall and clambered over awkwardly. By the time she dropped to the other side, Rafe had waded ankle deep into the mud.

'What can I do to help?' Caroline asked as he tossed his jacket to her. 'Tell me where the nearest farmhouse is and I'll run.'

'There's no time for that now. The sheep will die before you find the farmer, if you didn't get yourself lost on the way,' he barked. 'I told Stan the last time I saw him at market that he needed to repair that wall.' Rafe gestured to a part of the wall which had tumbled down. 'I told him that this field wasn't safe.'

'What can I do? I feel so useless.'

'If you stand there, a bit more to your left. That's fine. When I shout, hold your arms apart and walk slowly towards the gap in the fence.'

Caroline did so instantly.

'I don't see what being a useless scarecrow will do to help.'

'Fly and I will try to round them up. If they don't panic, we might be able to drive them back over the wall. Your scarecrow tactics will stop them heading off in that direction. We've done this sort of thing before.'

Caroline watched man and dog in action.

'Easy now.'

His voice was calm and soothing as the sheep bleated and struggled. Steadily, Rafe reached and pulled each one to safety. Caroline held her arms out and waved them slightly. The leading sheep took a long look at her and then stepped back over the wall. Caroline redoubled her efforts, making larger circles with her arms.

'Rafe, do you think this might do?'

Caroline started to drag a broken iron gate towards Rafe as he started to examine the wall.

'Good thinking.'

He rushed over and picked up the other end. It took a few seconds to place it over the gap where she held it while Rafe secured it in position with a few large stones.

'It will last for today.'

Rafe stepped back to examine their work.

'I'm not sure what I would have done without you and your quick thinking.'

Caroline felt a warm glow build inside her at his simple compliment. She ran and retrieved his coat from where she'd placed it. He took the coat and reached out, but Caroline stepped away.

'I'm sure you would have found a way, but thank you.'

She started to walk along the wall, pretending to look for a stile.

'Caroline, I need to find Stan. He needs to make that wall secure. Sorry about the walk, but this comes first.'

Caroline looked at the man, splattered with mud and grime.

'You did a good deed, Rafe Worthington. Those sheep would've died without your help.'

Rafe smiled back.

'It is something I expect any farmer would've done. Common courtesy, really.'

She wanted to hold him tight and tell him how worried she'd been when he was in the bog, but she contented herself with a smile.

'Walks can happen any time. It's the animals that are important. Let's find that farmer,' she said.

Later, sipping a mug of strong, milky tea in Stan's farmhouse kitchen, Caroline felt a well of happiness grow within her. Simple city girls had their uses! As quickly as the thought came, Caroline quashed it ruthlessly. Emotion had no place in this relationship, she reminded herself.

Caroline swallowed hard, and fought back the tears. The act of drinking the tea calmed her and after a few seconds she was able to look around the room again. Rafe did not mention the wall until after they had finished the tea, but then he spoke with a quiet force. Soon, Stan and his wife were nodding in agreement. 'Think if they had lost any more stock,' Caroline said as they walked back slowly towards the castle.

Stan had offered them a lift but Rafe refused.

'If only he'd listened the other two times,' Rafe answered shortly. 'I suspect you're right though, and he listened this time.'

Rafe smiled down at Caroline. Her breath caught in her throat as he leaned towards her. His hand hovered for a split second before he pushed a stray lock of hair from her face.

'Last one home is a rotten egg!'

He took off at a run with Fly yapping at his heels. Caroline put her hands on her hips. She wanted to scream in frustration.

'Wait, Rafe Worthington, you good-for-nothing cheat! You come back and start this race properly.'

'No, ma'am,' the joking answer came. 'If we did it your way, I'd never stand a chance.'

Fly barked excitedly and ran back and forth between the two as Caroline took off after Rafe up the hill to the castle. She ran as fast as she could, managing to catch up with him as he reached the driveway.

They arrived back at the castle breathless. Rafe put his hands on his knees. Caroline grabbed on to the door handle to support herself as she struggled to regain her breath.

Rafe watched her, his eyes deepening to an emerald green, but he made no move to touch her. Her lips parted but the door swung open, and Caroline jumped back.

'There you two are,' Jenna said with a triumphant note in her voice. 'Something special has arrived for you!'

Jenna's eyes became slits.

'Goodness, Caroline. What have you done to your trousers? I'm extraordinarily pleased I didn't go on that gentle stroll of yours. You've been gone three hours and look like you took a mud bath.'

Why am I putting myself through this, Caroline wondered, but replied calmly. 'Perhaps I ought to take a moment and get changed. If you'll excuse me,' she stammered.

'No, no, you must come in and open the package. I am sure Mrs Dodds will not mind mud on the carpet.'

Caroline felt Rafe's warm hand at her back and turned towards him. He gave her an encouraging smile.

'I think Caroline looks just fine. I like to see a woman rose-cheeked from the wind, and if I don't mind about the mud, Mrs Dodds is sure not to. Shall we go and see what this big surprise is about, Caroline?'

A large brown wrapped parcel stood in the centre of the drawing-room. Howard and Aunt Alice sat with expectant faces. Caroline noticed it was addressed in bold letters to Mr and Mrs Rafe Worthington.

'Should we open it now or wait?' Caroline tried to keep her voice light.

'Open now,' Jenna urged in a sweet tone. 'It's from Rafe's mother. She is desperately sorry she can't be here, but she has sent a special gift. From one artist to another.'

'Go ahead, Caroline,' Rafe said quietly but Caroline could hear the strain in his voice.

The Rafe who stood next to her was a very different man to the one who had raced with her. Caroline swallowed hard, and concentrated on removing the paper. In a few seconds an abstract painting in bright blazing pink was revealed. Caroline groped for words to express her feelings about the painting. It was jarring and vaguely offensive, the epitome of bad taste!

Caroline paid close attention to the pattern of the oriental carpet.

'I . . . uh . . . I don't know what to

say. It's such an unexpected gift.'

'What sort of joke is this, Jenna? You know I hate abstract painting,' Rafe said coldly.

Caroline lifted her eyes to see Rafe simmering with rage, his face red and his hands clenched at his sides.

'How kind of your mother to think of us,' she said quickly.

'You're not seriously saying that you like that painting?'

'It's a gift from your mother to celebrate our wedding.'

'Do what you like with it, just as long as I don't have to see it on a daily basis.'

Rafe left the room and slammed the door behind him.

'Oh, dear, I hope I haven't caused any problems,' Jenna said in a mock contrite voice.

★　★　★

'Everything is better after a hot shower,' Caroline said to Bertram, towelling off her hair.

She'd endured the tea for only a few minutes after Rafe had left. Now she had to start thinking about her own situation. Her main problem was not her lack of relationship with Rafe but where was she going to live and work after this holiday was finished, and how she was going to ensure Adams' Stitchery expanded and thrived.

She should never have left London. But now, she was trapped. How could she go through with this? How could she not go through with it? The sensible thing to do would be to go through with the ceremony, and leave as quickly as possible afterwards.

A knock on the door made her jump.

'Come in,' she called over her shoulder.

Rafe opened the door. Dressed in clean jeans, and dark green shirt, with his hair faintly damp, Caroline thought for a split second that somehow she'd conjured him up just thinking about him. She pulled the lapels of her bathrobe tighter, immediately conscious of his intense glance.

'You wanted something?'

Her words broke the spell, and Rafe stepped into the room, closing the door behind him. The scent of his aftershave filled her nostrils.

'I thought perhaps I ought to explain about my mother and the gift.'

'There's no need. I'm here to serve a purpose, not to get involved in family politics.'

'Still, I feel I owe you an explanation.' He held out his hands. 'It is the least I could do. My behaviour must seem very odd to you.'

'Why?'

'My mother and I . . . well . . . we don't get on. She gave me up as a child. I was an encumbrance she didn't need, an embarrassment. We have not seen each other since I refused to fund her lover's art gallery. She said if I would not give her money . . . '

'You don't need to tell me this.'

'I feel I must.'

He was now standing so close that

she only had to reach out a hand to touch him. Suddenly, her mobile rang. Rafe made a gesture towards it, and Caroline went and picked it up.

'Caroline here.'

She turned her back on Rafe, her mind instantly switching to business mode as she tried to anticipate what the next crisis would be.

When Caroline hung up, she felt like she was on autopilot. Everywhere she turned, more problems arose. Here was her head designer, Jules, offered another job in the same area. Caroline faced the very real prospect of losing her most senior designer, but without new premises, Caroline knew her chances of topping the offer made to her were slim.

'Is there something I can do?' Rafe asked.

Yes, hold me, her heart cried out.

'No, nothing. I can handle it. One of the designers who works for me has had another job offer.'

'If there is anything I can do . . . '

Caroline nodded. Her body felt as if it were encased in ice.

'I have to make a few phone calls. Would you mind if I didn't come down to dinner? I don't think I'm quite up to it.'

'Not a problem. I'll say you have a headache.'

She waited until he left the room, and threw herself full length on the bed, sobbing.

8

As Caroline walked to the woods the next morning, she thought about Rafe. Outside, they seemed to get along. However, when surrounded by other people, she felt like there was no hope. Their worlds were too different. His was landed gentry, hers was her needlework business.

She wanted there to be hope. She wanted this man to care about her.

She went to the rock where she had sat on the first morning and settled down to draw. Her sketches came thick and fast, and she began to expand on the dragon theme. Her hand stilled and she sat staring at the castle. She started to make a list of all the things she would have to do later in the week. Number one was to try to find a new office.

She bit the end of her pencil, and

drew a small cottage at the edge of a wood. Maybe she should consider leaving London altogether. It didn't matter where the business was located, and she might be able to get something for her flat, if it was still standing.

Northumberland might be interesting to relocate to. Its countryside was doing wonders for her creativity. The sight of Rafe striding with Fly back towards the castle without so much as a glance towards the rock where she was sitting rapidly brought her to her senses. She looked at her list, and then crumpled it up. She wasn't thinking straight. She was trying to find excuses to stay.

'He isn't going to like you any better if you camp on his doorstep. You'll be an embarrassment, a reminder of an episode he'd rather forget,' she whispered to herself.

The sun went behind a cloud and Caroline began to pack up her sketching equipment. She was almost back at the castle when her arm was grabbed.

She turned and faced not Rafe, but Howard.

'I want to talk with you, Caroline Adams of Adams' Stitchery. I have a proposition for you.'

Caroline turned, her mouth dropping open in surprise.

'What are you talking about?'

'This will only take a few minutes of your time, and they may well be the most important few minutes of your career.'

He led Caroline a little way away from the castle, to a stone bench.

'You own Adams' Stitchery, do you not?'

'I've never hidden the fact,' she said.

'I've been checking up on you, finding out what sort of person will be joining our little family. I received the report this morning. You're a very interesting young lady, if I may say so.'

Caroline felt her anger grow. How dare he check up on her! What gave him the right!

'I happen to know, for instance, you

will be needing a new place of work soon. You're behind on your rent, Ms Adams.'

'I think you'll find your information is incorrect.'

Caroline hoped Margo had remembered to put the cheque she had left in the post.

'As I'm moving up here, what happens in London is of little concern.'

'Still playing the party line, are you? Let me make you an offer. Leave Rafe standing at the altar and I will see to it personally that you find a new office at the price you are looking for in my new development. I also might be able to see my way clear to making sure that loan you applied for goes through without a hitch. The bank manager is, shall we say, a friend.'

'Why on earth should I take you up on that offer?' Caroline spat out.

'Because you're not some muddle-headed fool.'

'I regret that I must decline your offer. I hope you didn't pay money for that report on me, as it is not worth even the paper it is written on.'

She turned her back and started to walk rapidly towards the castle. Her lip hurt from where she bit it. The man was a reptile. Somebody had to stand up to him. If anything, his words had made her more determined.

'Caroline, the offer stands,' he called. 'When you've thought about it, I'm confident you'll see it my way, being the astute businesswoman you are.'

She heard his voice calling, but her steps didn't falter as she walked quickly towards the castle. Once inside Caroline stopped outside the study. If she took Howard's sleazy offer, there was every chance things would go on as before. Adams' Stitchery would continue much as it had. She'd put too much time and effort into building this business to let it fail, but how could she look at herself in the mirror, knowing she had sold someone she cared about for pieces of silver?

She sighed and knocked at the door.

At the sound of the knock, Rafe turned from the computer. Anything was a welcome distraction from his thoughts of Caroline. She made it quite clear that she wasn't interested in him or his family problems. Her thoughts were only for her business, just like his mother.

'Come in,' he called in response to the second knock.

The door creaked open and there was Caroline, standing uncertainly in the doorway, and he knew his resolve was weak.

Caroline swallowed as she sat down. Now that she was here in his inner sanctum, she had to explain her problem, but the words refused to come.

'Is there something wrong, Caroline?'

He came over and kneeled by her chair.

'If there is anything I can do, let me know. Think of me as your friend, a big brother, and confide in me.'

He laid a warm hand on her cold

ones. She lifted her eyes to meet his, and watched his face blur slightly. Rafe as a big brother was the last thing she wanted. She knew that, but it was all he was offering.

'Howard knows about us, about the plan, about everything,' she whispered.

He released her hand and went to stand by the window.

'He has employed a private detective to find out about me and my business,' she continued.

'It's not exactly a secret, is it?'

'No, I never made a secret of what I did. What is new is he has offered me a place for my office, if I don't marry you, an offer I'd be a fool to refuse. It's for a loan, the office, everything.'

'And what did you say?'

Caroline looked at the set line of his shoulders, but she could tell nothing from it. Did her problems matter at all to him or was she only a means to an end?

'I refused,' she whispered.

Rafe was back by her side in an instant.

'You refused? Why?'

She wanted to tell him the real reason she refused, but the words stuck in her throat. Her lips parted, aching to feel his mouth on hers, but she pressed them tightly together. Big brother, he had said.

'I don't like his methods,' she said. 'He's a reptile of the first order. I don't trust him. He could easily turn round and throw my studio and me out in the street after I'd given what he wants. I dislike bribery.'

His eyes became hooded, and he dropped a hand on her shoulder.

'Thank goodness for that. I knew I could trust you.'

'If I had done what he wanted, I could have ended up without a studio anyway. He's hardly likely to put his offer in writing, and besides, you are going to help me find financing. That was part of the deal.'

Rafe picked up a pen and toyed with

it. The deal . . . the loan . . . the money. It always came back to it. She wasn't interested in him, only what his wealth and status could do for her. Why couldn't he accept that Caroline was from the same mould as his mother? And just like his mother, she'd abandoned him. But she isn't, she can't be, was the immediate answer from his heart. She is here, telling you about it, not high-tailing it in her car back to London.

'I meant what I said. I will help you out with the money.'

She stood up, wiping her hands on her jeans.

'I thought you should know. Who knows what he might try next.'

'You are still willing to marry me, to go through with the ceremony?'

Rafe held his breath and waited. Caroline closed her eyes. There were a thousand reasons why she should refuse, sensible reasons like keeping her business together and not changing her life. But her heart wasn't listening. It kept repeating the one reason, the only reason why she'd marry him — to give him his heart's desire, the castle.

'No reason, none that I can think of. We're friends now and friends don't let each other down. Why?'

She forced her voice to be bright and cheery.

'It's been a long day. Tomorrow is going to be an even longer one. I think I'd best say good-night.'

'Aren't you going to give me a good-night kiss?' he asked, his eyes darkening.

Caroline stopped. It was the one thing she wanted most in the world but also feared. There was only one place it would lead — heartbreak. She wasn't ready for a casual affair, not even with him. She wanted more.

'I don't think it would be a good idea under the circumstances.'

'What do you mean?'

'It's not as if we are attracted to each other,' she lied. 'It is a mutually-beneficial relationship. You get the castle, and I get a chance to expand my company without having to crawl to some reptile like Howard Steel.'

'As you say. By the way, tomorrow night, I think it would be best if we did share a bedroom. I wouldn't want any more threats from Steel. I suspect unless he and Jenna are convinced our marriage is real, they will try to cause trouble. Sweet dreams.'

★ ★ ★

Caroline tried once more to get her hair to stay in place. So far this morning, she'd washed it, dried it, sprayed it and it still insisted on doing its own thing. Why today of all days would she have to have a bad hair day?

She looked at the wedding hat, lying in its bed of tissue. Two days ago, when her hair was behaving itself, it had seemed the perfect finishing touch to the white dress. Today, the hat made her look like a clown. She couldn't wear it and maintain any self-respect.

She pressed her lips together tightly, and redoubled her efforts. The small plastic travel clock said nine twenty-five. The appointment with the registrar was ten o'clock. She regarded herself in the mirror. If it wasn't elegant, at least it wasn't Coco the Clown or the Bride of Frankenstein either. But her heart still felt heavy. All night her sleep had been full of nightmares.

How could she enter into a loveless, cold marriage, and knowing what she knew, how could she not?

'Caroline? Are you ready to go?' Rafe called through the door.

Her hand trembled as she pulled open the door. Rafe stood in the dim hallway, dressed in a navy blue striped suit with a light blue shirt and green striped tie. His aftershave smelled of roses, lavender and rosemary, reeking of sophistication and old money.

She knew that he was only dressing like that in order to fool his relatives into thinking the marriage was real, but her heart wanted to believe he had made an effort for her.

'Give me a twirl.'

He made a small circle with his hands and looked at her with unfathomable eyes. She turned round obediently, feeling her face burn.

'I was hoping not to look like I had stuck my finger in a light socket, but my hair had other ideas,' she said with a short laugh, struggling for humour.

He reached out and smoothed a rebellious tendril of hair. He smiled slightly, and pushed another strand back from her forehead.

She swallowed and tried to get hold of herself. She wanted to marry him but not like this. She wanted it to be real. All her earlier hopes of Jenna exploding seemed so ridiculous now. She couldn't back out and yet how could she go forward?

'I'd best take a tissue. I always seem to cry at weddings.'

'Are you going to go through with this?'

She could feel his breath on her

cheek. She tightened her jaw and refused to let her doubts overwhelm her.

'I told you I would, and I mean to keep my promise. Everything that has happened only reinforced my decision.'

'I can't tell you how much this means to me, what you are about to do. You have my deep appreciation.'

He looked at her with an unfathomable look in his eyes. For an instant, Caroline thought she saw hurt, but it was gone almost before she could think what it was.

It was hard to describe what Rafe felt when he opened the door and saw her in her bridal clothes. With the sun shining through her hair, it looked like she was wearing a halo. He remembered telling Uncle Jack years ago that when he married, he was going to marry an angel. An angel was probably the best description he could come up with for Caroline.

He wasn't sure what he'd done to deserve her, even for a few days. Last night, he had thought about trying to persuade her to stay, to make this marriage real but he feared her response. There would come a time when she'd decide to go, much like his mother had done with his father. All his life, he had failed to understand how his father could have given in to such despair about a woman leaving him. Then he met Caroline and he knew if he let himself, he could begin to love her with such a passion.

'Oh, there you two are. We were beginning to wonder if one or both of you had cold feet.'

His cousin called to them as they walked slowly down the stairs. Rafe kept his hand on Caroline's elbow, in part to help her, and in part because he could not stop himself from using the smallest excuse to touch her.

'Just a bit of bother with my hair,' Caroline called down. 'Besides, it's the bride's prerogative to be a bit late.'

His cousin tossed the end of her shawl over her shoulder.

'Are you sure it's proper for the bride to travel with the groom? We have plenty of room, if you want to go with us, Caroline.'

Caroline looked at Jenna with her smug grin and perfect hairdo. She glanced back at Rafe. Her hands trembled.

'No, it's fine. I'm not into superstitions. At least with Rafe, I'll be sure of getting there on time.' She gave a little laugh. 'A good start to a happy marriage.'

She wanted to believe that. She offered prayers to anyone who might be listening that somehow that might be the case, that this marriage would be more than a sham. She moved slowly towards the large oak door, stopping to give a nervous smile to Aunt Alice.

'If you need a good lawyer after the ceremony, I know several,' Jenna hissed in her ear but Caroline kept her cool.

'I don't know what you are talking about.'

The time had finally come. She had to say something. She could no longer carry on this charade. She was about to betray her dream of a marriage to help the man she loved, but Aunt Alice deserved the truth.

'Still playing the love-struck fiancée, are we?' Jenna's smile was nasty, more like a grimace. 'I didn't actually think you'd go through with it, but there's no accounting for desperation, is there? But you can't seriously think my cousin is going to stay married to you.'

'Whatever are you talking about Jenna?' Aunt Alice asked.

'Take a look at her. She has no dress sense, no money and has a dull, uninteresting little job. Why would he want to stay married to someone like her?' Jenna spat out, her face contorted with rage. 'He doesn't love you. How could you possibly think he loves you? This is all about his retaining control of the castle and spiting me, don't you understand?'

'Is this true, Rafe? Caroline?' Aunt Alice asked, turning from Jenna, her elderly face creased with concern.

9

Caroline fought to keep control. She wanted to tell the truth. She had to tell the truth, even if it put her in a bad light and made her seem like a heartless mercenary. She had to explain why she had been about to do this, and why she no longer could go through with it.

'It's the truth,' Caroline whispered.

She couldn't look at Rafe.

'Aunt Alice, your nephew loves this castle and estate so much he was prepared to accept me as his bride. We haven't known each other very long, but what I know of him, I know to be good and true. He is the sort of man with whom I would be proud to spend the rest of my life.'

'Let me tell you what I think about the cheap, shoddy trick you and my cousin have played and are trying to play,' Jenna squawked. 'This castle is mine. Howard and I have great plans for this heap of rocks, and I will see this castle turned into a holiday centre if that is the last thing I do.'

'I've no idea what you are talking about, but I think you had better leave.'

Caroline's voice was low but very determined. She was quite ready to pick the woman up and throw her out the door.

'I never asked you why you married your husband.'

'Yes, Jenna, I think perhaps it would be best if you left,' Aunt Alice said firmly. 'I have no wish for this castle to be turned into some sort of amusement arcade. It is more than a pile of rocks. It is the cornerstone of my family and I want it to go to someone who cares about it and cherishes it, not someone who wants to destroy it.'

Jenna's mouth dropped open. Caroline struggled to keep her face straight.

'Howard and I will be off in a few minutes. We know when we are not wanted. I can't bear staying in this draughty pile of broken-down rocks a moment longer,' Jenna burst out.

'So, you reveal your true feelings at last,' Rafe said coldly.

Jenna flushed.

'I . . . well . . . that is, I don't think the country is really all that healthy. Howard, are you ready? Let's shake this dust from our feet.'

'Aren't you taking Aunt Alice with you? You can't abandon an eighty-year-old woman.' Rafe sounded incredulous.

'If she wants this pile of rocks, she should stay here and find her own way home.'

Jenna stalked out of the room. Howard hurried after her.

'Good riddance.' Aunt Alice sniffed. 'To think I actually thought she had changed.'

'She fooled us all,' Rafe said. 'Aunt Alice, don't worry. You can stay with me for as long as you like. However, I think the marriage should be postponed for a little while.'

'I agree,' Aunt Alice said. 'We had

enough of this hole-in-the-corner marriage with your father. Caroline deserves a proper white wedding, and she deserves a bridegroom who is marrying her for more than a piece of land. My half of the castle is yours, Rafe.'

Caroline stared at Rafe. She didn't know what to say. There seemed to be little reason for her to stay now. There was no reason for them to marry either. She would be an unwelcome reminder. She opened her mouth, just as Mrs Dodds came into the breakfast room.

'John Miles is on the phone. He'd like a word with you, Mr Worthington.'

'We need to talk,' Rafe said quietly to Caroline before he answered the phone. 'But not now. Wait until Jenna and Howard leave. You did wonderfully.'

Caroline bit her lip and nodded. He'd want to make arrangements for the loan before she left. It would be easier that way. Saying goodbye to him was going to be one of the hardest things she'd ever done in her life. Caroline was still sitting nursing her cup of coffee when Rafe returned from his phone call. For half a second, he was tempted to ask her to come with him, but he wanted to have their talk alone. He had so many things to say to her.

'I have to go out, but it shouldn't take long.'

She shrugged and played with her toast.

'That's fine. There are a number of things I need to do, things I need to pack.'

Rafe reached out a hand towards her before letting it fall to his side. If he took her in his arms, he wouldn't reach the farm in time.

'This shouldn't take long. Then we'll talk.'

'I'll be here.'

'I'm counting on that.'

Two hours later, up at the farm, the vet gave the provisional all-clear. It looked like a simple case of foot rot. Rafe felt a large weight roll off his back. This time it was a false alarm. He praised Jim for his quick reactions and eagle eyes, but reminded him to take more care in the future.

He whistled to Fly and started to walk back towards the castle. With any luck, Caroline would be alone, and they could have a serious discussion about their future. Rafe smiled as he thought of how she helped to rescue the stranded sheep without questioning. For some reason fate seemed to have dealt him a winning hand this time when Ms Adams had showed up on his doorstep.

Rafe quickened his pace as he walked back to the castle. The sun was shining, the landscape was sparkling, and it was a new day for the taking. Caroline would be there, Jenna and Howard wouldn't be and somehow, some way, he was going to make sure she knew he loved her and convince her that he was the best man for her. He flung his arms wide to embrace the world and Fly looked at him as if he'd lost his mind.

Rafe picked up a stick and tossed it

for Fly who obligingly chased it. The high walk along the ridge had been a favourite of his since he was a boy. Fly dropped the stick and danced lightly in front of him. Rafe stepped to one side, and suddenly the bank gave way, sending him tumbling head over heels down the bank. He hit his head on a rock, turned over twice more then lay still.

★   ★   ★

After Jenna and Howard drove off, their car spewing up gravel as if they were in a race to escape, Caroline changed into jeans and her sweatshirt. She tried to pack, but kept finding excuses for why she should stay. Perhaps she should stay for another day until she knew she had a home to return to.

Her mood lightened with the thought and she hurried off to see if Rafe had returned, but the first person she found was Mrs Dodds.

'Has Rafe come back?' she asked.

'No, miss.' The housekeeper turned to face Caroline. 'I haven't seen him since he left for the farm.'

'Do you think he'll be long?'

'He shouldn't be much longer. I wouldn't worry, miss, he'll be back as soon as he possibly can be. Pity about the wedding, but good riddance to bad rubbish, I say. I never liked her. You can marry in your own sweet time now.'

Caroline pressed her lips together. Until she had spoken with Rafe, she had to keep pretending.

'Do you think something could have happened to him?' she asked, trying to divert Mrs Dodds' attention.

The housekeeper shook her head.

'Mr Rafe? No. He knows the estate like the back of his hand. He'll turn up right as rain, in a little while.'

Unable to settle, Caroline went out on to the gravel drive. She was just turning back to the castle, when an exhausted Fly came bounding up the hill. Caroline shaded her eyes. No Rafe!

'Has something happened, Fly?'

The dog barked, and grabbed a trouser leg, trying to pull Caroline towards the woods.

'OK, OK,' Caroline said and stroked Fly's head. 'I get the message.'

She walked over to the castle and opened the door.

'Mrs Dodds, Aunt Alice,' she called, 'I think something has happened to Rafe. Fly is here on his own. I think he wants me to follow him.'

'Do slow down, Fly,' Caroline called as she tried to pick her way carefully through the undergrowth as the dog raced ahead.

Every so often, Fly doubled back and barked at Caroline. Once he caught her sweater in his teeth and tried to pull her forwards. Caroline paused for a breath, one hand against a tree, wondering if she should turn back, before it became too late.

Then she saw him, sitting propped up against a tree, with a gash on the side of his forehead. At the sound of her voice, Rafe looked up and gave a wan smile. Even from where she was standing, Caroline could see the traces of dirt and perhaps blood on his face. He started to try to stand up.

'Don't bother, I'm coming down,' she called, gingerly stepping off the path, and hugging a tree.

'Be careful,' Rafe called back. 'It's a nasty drop.'

'I can see that.'

Caroline began to pick her way down, hanging on to branches, trying to lurch from one tree trunk to another. At one point, the slippery moss on the rocks forced Caroline to slide a short way on her bottom.

Rafe struggled to an upright position when she was almost beside him. He grimaced as he tried to put weight on his left foot.

'You needn't have done that,' he said as Caroline reached him. 'I can manage all right on my own.'

'Yeah, right,' she said, putting her hands on her hips. 'How exactly were you planning to climb back up that hill?'

A trace of a smile played on his lips.

'I was working on that.'

'Presuming you did climb the hill, do you realise how far you'll have to walk? So quit trying to be a hero and accept some help for a change,' Caroline said in mock exasperation.

'You're right, I could use a bit of help,' Rafe admitted, grudgingly. 'Are you going to stand there, looking pretty or are you going to help?'

'Compliments will get you everywhere,' she retorted, holding out her hand.

He grabbed it, using her to steady himself. Caroline was conscious of his height, his presence, his very nearness. His hand felt cold in hers. They stood for a few seconds, staring at each other quietly. Her legs felt limp and the butterflies in her stomach started to fly about. She felt if she didn't hold on to something, her legs would give way. She slipped her hand out of his grasp, and grabbed a tree branch.

Rafe tried to put his weight on his

right foot. He grunted slightly.

'Is it painful?' Caroline asked and wished immediately she hadn't asked. From the pained expression on Rafe's face, she knew she'd asked the obvious.

'Of course it's painful.'

He tried to walk on the injured leg, putting one hand on her shoulder and managed to hop.

'It's not broken, which is something.'

'Will you be able to walk to the castle or should I go get some help?'

She looked up the slope and tried to remember the way back to the castle.

'I can walk, with a bit of help from you. Just don't leave.'

Caroline nodded. She didn't need much encouragement to stay. She hadn't wanted to leave him on his own, particularly as she wasn't sure how she was going to find this place again.

'Shall I find you a branch to lean on?'

Caroline started to hunt around the undergrowth. There were several small sticks but nothing big or sturdy enough for Rafe to use as a crutch.

'I think I can manage with an arm.'

Caroline glanced up at the steep hillside. How was she going to get him back up there? She felt a stab of panic.

'Is there an easier way?' Caroline asked, trying for a light-hearted approach. 'To be honest with you, I don't fancy a climb up that hill. My shoes are not up to it.'

Rafe pointed down the ravine.

'If we go along here for a bit, an ancestor of mine built a series of stairs.'

Caroline dropped her gaze. She so desperately wanted to tell him about how she felt, but somehow could not bring herself to say the words. Would he even believe them if she did or would he think she only said them out of pity.

'We really need to get back,' she said. 'Howard and Jenna have gone.'

He winced slightly as he tried to put more weight on his foot.

'I can't pretend to be sorry. In the end, Jenna revealed her true colours, as I predicted.'

'Are you sure you don't want me to get some help?'

She refused to think about what was going to happen when they arrived back and she had to walk out of his life for ever. She couldn't stay, not with her heart in danger the way it was. With the slightest encouragement, she'd beg him to marry her.

'Positive,' Rafe grunted. 'Now come here and lend a shoulder.'

Caroline went over to Rafe. She hesitated for a second before she put her arm about his waist. She drew strength from Rafe's closeness. They moved in tandem, slowly but determinedly.

'How bad is the ankle? Do you need to go to hospital?'

'It's only a slight sprain.'

He smiled a tight smile, and used his free hand to ruffle Caroline's hair, picking out one or two twigs.

'I'll tape it up when we get back. Don't fuss.'

Caroline felt the warmth start in her

stomach and spread through her body. This was where she wanted to be, where she wanted to stay. Her mouth started to form the words, but she paused, unable to say them. She couldn't say anything, until she knew how he felt. The embarrassment of a one-sided love affair would be too great and she concentrated on where she put her feet.

Mrs Dodds was sitting in the hallway with her handbag at her feet, when they finally reached home. She got to her feet and offered a hand as Caroline helped Rafe through the door. He waved both of them away.

'I'm not an invalid, you know.'

Caroline answered Mrs Dodds' questioning look with a shrug.

'Unless you want a quick trip to the hospital, you need to rest your ankle.'

Mrs Dodds picked up her handbag and started to go out the door.

'I've made a steak and kidney pie, and put it along with some baked potatoes in the bottom oven. Are you sure he's going to be all right?' she finished in a low voice to Caroline.

'I wish people would stop fussing over me like I was some sort of accident victim. I can assure you, Mrs Dodds, it is no more than a scratch, and a twisted ankle. You get home to your grandchildren. Tuesday's the day you look after them, isn't it?'

He closed the door with a loud bang after Mrs Dodds went through. Caroline glanced at him, her lips parted to ask if he wanted to eat, but the words died on her lips when she saw his white pinched face.

'You ought to get to bed. You're not well.'

'Didn't Mrs Dodds say she'd left a few things for a late lunch? It shouldn't take long to fix something to eat.'

He started towards the kitchen. Caroline ran around him and blocked his way. If she was going to play nurse, then it was her responsibility. Besides, she wasn't quite sure what she was going to do if he collapsed in a heap.

'You ought to rest.'

'Stop fussing.' Rafe put a hand on his forehead and wiped away the sweat. 'I told you I'm fine. I'm simply tired. I haven't had much sleep.'

'If fine is practically fainting, then I'd believe you, but as we both know, you are far from fine.' Caroline put her hands on her hips. 'You do no-one any good by this invincible act.'

'The meal will only take two minutes to fix,' Rafe pleaded.

'If you get yourself into bed, I'll dish it up. Even a non-cooking genius like me can work out how to dish food on a plate. Now go! You are not wanted here.'

'I thought you were supposed to be keeping an eye on me.'

He swayed slightly, and closed his eyes.

'Are you feeling worse?' She moved closer to him in case she had to break his fall. 'We can always go to the hospital.'

'I told you, I hate hospitals,' Rafe

said. 'People go there to die.'

'Oh, stop being melodramatic. You twisted your ankle.'

The minute she said the words, she wished she could unsay them. Rafe was obviously not well. He was very pale, and the beads of sweat were back on his forehead. She made a decision. Food could wait.

'I think we'd best get you in bed first.'

Her voice was quieter, gentler.

'Why?'

Caroline tried to keep her temper. Arguing with an invalid was not a good idea.

'Because I think it would be a good idea.'

'Will you be joining me?' Rafe asked, teasingly.

Caroline's heart leaped and her colour rose.

'I rather think you have had enough exercise for today.'

Rafe's eyes deepened to an emerald green, and he smiled a half smile.

'So that is what it is called these days. I had best remember it.'

Caroline wanted to think of a crushing reply, but none came. Instead she walked towards the bedroom corridor, her head held high.

'Caroline.' Rafe was at her side in an instant. He grabbed her arm. 'Caroline, sweetheart, I didn't mean to offend you.'

Caroline looked into the deep green eyes, the eyes that had become so clear to her so quickly.

'You didn't offend me,' she replied, her voice barely above a whisper.

Caroline's lips parted as Rafe brought his head towards hers. His mouth was every bit as sweet as she remembered. Instantly, she put her arms around him. Rafe crushed her to his chest. She wanted the kiss to last for ever. In his arms, she had no doubts. She did not want to think, to worry or to wonder, she wanted to feel.

A slight groan from Rafe brought Caroline crashing back to earth and she stepped out of his arms.

'Whatever are we doing? Kissing on the stairs like a couple of teenagers.'

She set off down the hall and then turned to see if he was following.

'You need to be in bed, my friend, for rest.'

Rafe made a noise.

'There is no good protesting.' She put her hands on her hips. 'However, one more word from you about me helping and I will take you straight to hospital.'

She moved Bertram on to the armchair and folded back the covers of the bed.

'Where do you keep your night clothes?'

She went over to his chest of drawers, pulling out the top drawer. She needed to be doing something to keep her mind occupied.

'As a general rule of thumb, I don't wear any,' the laconic reply came from the doorway.

Caroline gulped, her hands frozen in

mid-air as the image of Rafe in all his glory flashed in front of her eyes.

'You'll get cold in bed.'

'Not if you were there beside me.'

His voice held a different, warmer note.

Caroline peeped at Rafe from under her eyelashes.

'That wouldn't be a very good idea,' she said after a minute.

She slid the drawer back and started towards the door.

'Why ever not?' Rafe took a step towards her.

They were standing so close that she could reach out and touch his chest if she wanted to. She reached out a hand. It hovered there for an instant before she clasped both hands together.

'Because it wouldn't, that's why. It would complicate matters.'

Rafe took a step closer. There was a hair's breadth between their bodies. The scent of his aftershave filled her nostrils. He reached out a hand. His forefinger pushed back a lock of hair.

'How complicate?' he asked with a low, husky voice that sent shivers down her spine.

Unable to resist, Caroline turned her head and kissed his palm.

'Trust me, it would.'

Rafe lifted her chin and she could see the darkening pools of green.

'Tell me the truth, Caroline. Do you want to stay beside me tonight as much as I want you to?'

She wanted to make a smart remark. She wanted to retain a small piece of herself. She did not want Rafe to know her true feelings about him, about them. She opened her mouth, but no sound emerged. She closed her eyes, and shook her head. A single tear ran down her cheek.

His finger caught the tear and brought it to his lips. He kissed the finger and gently laid it back on her cheek.

'I asked you to tell me the truth.'

He gathered her into his arms. All her doubts and fears vanished but a little voice in the back of her head told her the longer she stayed, the harder it would be for her to leave.

Rafe winced slightly, and covered her hand with his. He brought her hand to his lips, kissing the palm gently, his tongue teasing each finger in turn.

Caroline looked into his eyes and saw the brief flash of pain.

'I am so sorry,' Caroline exclaimed, breaking the spell.

She hurried out of his arms, over to the bed, and busied herself with pulling back the covers, and plumping the pillows, anything, anything at all to hide her confusion.

'Caroline.'

She turned at the sound of her name. Her tongue flicked over her dry lips. Rafe was standing where she had left him, looking somehow alone and vulnerable. Her hands still held the last pillow. Mechanically, she replaced the pillow on the bed.

Her heart told her to run to him, and

kiss away the hurt, but her legs wouldn't move.

'I . . . I think . . . '

She paused, and tried to think of how best she could get out this situation with her dignity intact.

'I really think you ought to get cleaned up a bit. Your face has streaks of mud on it. In the meantime, I will get lunch.'

She rushed the last words before she backed out of the door.

In the hallway, she stood, her chest heaving for a few seconds, trying to regain her composure. She heard a short laugh from the room as she sprinted down the hall, away from the sound, her face burning.

10

As Caroline had hoped, Rafe was in bed with his eyes closed when she returned with the tray. She resisted the temptation to kiss his forehead and smooth the bedclothes. The cups clinked slightly as she set the tray carefully on the table.

Rafe gave a slight moan in his sleep, and Caroline glanced at him. Her breath caught in her throat. The bedclothes had slipped and his naked chest was exposed. For several heartbeats, she watched it rise and fall with each breath he took.

She took a step backwards. He gave another moan, a mumbled word. The room swam before her eyes, and she tasted the salt of the unshed tears in her mouth. She was in love with him. She knew that now for certain.

For that reason, it was impossible to

stay. Love was not part of their bargain. Her one-sided love could only complicate matters. In order for their partnership to work, there had to be no tears when the time came to end it. The tears and the hurt were now inevitable.

Rafe mumbled slightly in his sleep, and stretched out a hand towards her. One kiss to the forehead would wake the sleeping prince, her heart told her. She swayed towards him, thinking of his earlier words asking her to stay with him. Her heart whispered that she would be cherished, loved.

What was going to happen when she asked more of him than he was prepared to give, her mind questioned. Could she face that? Could she face the reality that Rafe might want her for a little while, but ultimately he would discard her and her love?

She didn't want to find out that his passion did not match hers. Caroline bit her lip to hold back the sobs. No, she decided, ignoring her body's reaction to Rafe's nearness, it was better to leave like a thief in the night than to face rejection in the cold, clear light of day.

For half a minute, gazing at his still form, she was tempted to remain. If he'd woken or shown some sign of missing her, she'd have run to his arms, but he made no sign, and turned over.

A slight sparkle on her finger caught her eye. She swore softly as she remembered his ring. She tiptoed over to the bedside table, and froze as Rafe mumbled again in his sleep. Caroline slipped off the ring and placed it on the table. Her finger felt light and naked. She took one last look at Rafe's sleeping form, imprinting the image on her mind for ever.

'Farewell, my sweet prince,' she whispered softly before leaving the room.

Back in the relative safety of her own room, Caroline sat on the bed, her hands placed firmly on her thighs, breathing as if she had run a marathon. She leaned her head back slightly and contemplated her next action. She felt dreadful leaving. There were so many reasons for staying — she had promised the doctor for one, but then there were so many more compelling reasons for going.

'What if his words, his caresses were only down to his head injuries and the painkillers? What if he didn't mean them? What if he rejects me?' Caroline gasped as she tried to put Bertram in his cat carrier.

Through her tears, she tried unsuccessfully to close the cat carrier's door. The lump in her throat grew bigger as she imagined what it would be like to face a disbelieving, cold Rafe over breakfast. She could not bear the image of him rejecting her advances.

Caroline redoubled her efforts to get Bertram in his cage. After the initial protest, the cat blinked and, sleepy-eyed, offered no resistance.

In less than ten minutes, Caroline was dressed and ready. She penned a note swiftly.

Had to go. Love, Caroline.

Caroline crossed out the word 'love' and wrote instead, 'Best wishes'. It was inadequate, but it had to do. She shook her head and left the note on her bed, with the key.

Caroline packed her suitcase and Bertram into the car. Right before she got into the car, she took one last, lingering look at the castle. Was there a shadow of a man in the upstairs window? Caroline blinked her eyes, clearing the tears. The shadow was gone. It had to have been a trick of the light, she told herself as she put the key in the ignition.

★ ★ ★

In the three weeks after Caroline fled Haydon Castle, she spent much of the time remembering what might have been.

She had driven as fast as she dared, her vision blurred with unshed tears. By the time she reached the motorway, she had convinced herself she had done the right thing. When she turned the car into the street where her flat was, in the steel grey light of dawn, Caroline was struck by the terrible knowledge of what she had done.

By that time, it was too late. A new day had begun, and people were starting to move about. She couldn't just return and pretend it never happened. She wanted to, but she knew she couldn't. She desperately wanted to roll back the hours, and stay within the safety of Rafe's arms, but it was impossible.

For a week, she pretended that Rafe would call, come after her declaring his undying love then would decide that she was better off without him.

Halfway through the second week, she stopped lying to herself. Caroline knew that the mess she was in was entirely of her own making. Nothing seemed important, not the news that the planning application had been withdrawn abruptly and that Steel

Developments was being investigated for trying to bribe a planning officer; or that one of her kits had reached the top ten best-selling kits on the US; or even that the bank manager had reconsidered the loan application and it was now approved and that Adams' Stitchery could expand.

Everything seemed to pale into insignificance when she thought about Rafe.

Finally, at the beginning of the third week, she could stand it no longer. She tried phoning the castle — once, twice, three, four, five times.

She threw the handset back on the receiver each time and five minutes later, arms shaking, she dialled again. After the second ring, she placed the phone down as if it burned her and collapsed in a heap. She couldn't do this.

The next day, her hand trembling, she picked up the phone and started to dial. With each number, she took another breath. Sweat pricked at the back of her neck. This time the phone was picked up on the first ring.

'Worthington.'

Her heart lurched at the sound of his voice.

'Rafe, I . . . I'm sorry,' she whispered before she lost her nerve and slammed the phone down.

A few seconds later, it rang. Caroline stretched out a hand to pick it up but she couldn't. She hugged her knees and listened to it ring.

Later, after it finally fell silent and she decided to face her life, she sat down with a cup of coffee. Her hand knocked against a pile of papers, sending them flying, revealing a smooth stone, the stone she'd picked up that first morning. She reached out and held it in the palm of her hand.

If only, she thought, I could be given a second chance.

The doorbell rang, bringing Caroline to her senses. She must have dozed off, she realised, checking her watch. The bell rang again, insistent, impatient.

Caroline shuffled towards the door, opening it.

There, standing in the doorway was Rafe, thinner than she remembered but his eyes as deep green as ever. Caroline swallowed. She stepped back. She could not help noticing every detail of his appearance, from his immaculate navy blue overcoat to the shadows above his cheekbones. She wanted to stand there, drinking in his appearance.

'Are you going to ask me in?'

The muscles in his jaw clenched and unclenched as he waited for her answer.

'Of course,' she said, trying to smile. 'Come in, come in. But just for a moment. I'm about to go out.'

Rafe strode in, the long strides of a man with a purpose. Caroline was acutely conscious of the mess in her flat. She moved a pile of drawings and gestured to the sofa. He shook his head.

'It will only take a moment, but we need to talk.'

'How are your mother and aunt?'

Caroline hated herself for asking such

a banal question.

'They're fine. My mother is enjoying her time with Aunt Alice, I believe.'

'Did my leaving cause any problems? It hasn't affected you inheriting the castle, has it?'

'My mother did have a few words to say on the subject, more like a few home truths. But in answer to your second question, the castle is still mine.'

Caroline bit her lip, and did not meet his eye.

'I was wrong. I shouldn't have left the way I did.'

Rafe said nothing for a while. The silence stretched and engulfed the room. Caroline could hear his breathing, echoing hers. She glanced up at him. His entire body seemed poised, waiting for something more.

Caroline could not prevent the tears from falling down her cheeks. She didn't even try. She had left it much too late. There was no second chances not in real life, not with this man.

'I'm sorry,' she said to the floor and

the silence stretched Caroline's nerves to breaking point.

'I brought the drawings you left. I only found them yesterday. Mrs Dodds had put them in a drawer for safekeeping. I thought you might need them.'

Rafe held out the bundle stiffly.

'You said you needed them for your book. I didn't want you to have problems on account of . . . on account of . . . '

'I finished the book and the bank reconsidered. They've offered me a loan.'

'I could have saved myself a journey then.'

His voice held a note of coldness as he placed the drawings in a heap on the sofa.

'Is that what you are saying?'

'I'm not saying anything.'

Caroline couldn't bear it any longer. She threw herself at him, weeping. For several minutes, they stood there, Caroline no longer trying to hide her feelings. Rafe's arms tightened convulsively around her.

'Somebody's hurt you very badly, Caroline, hasn't he?'

He used his finger to raise her chin. Caroline looked into the deepening pools of green. The only thing he'd feel for her was pity. Poor, deluded girl, he'd probably think.

'Why would you ask that?' she whispered.

'Caroline, are you going to tell me what's wrong?'

'It was very kind of you to bring back my drawings,' she said, trying to change the subject.

Rafe grasped Caroline by the shoulders, and forced her to look at him.

'You are not going to get away so easily this time. You phoned me. Don't deny it. Something is wrong, and I think I have a right to know what it is.'

'You.'

Her voice was barely audible. She had reached the end of the road. There was no denying it. She was not sure that she'd wake up and find this whole thing a dream. She raised a hand to flick a stray piece of hair out of his eyes.

'I was frightened,' Caroline said directly to his chest. 'When my family died, I made a vow that I would never allow anyone to get that close again. The pain of their loss was too great. Then you happened and I forgot about keeping you at a distance.'

'Caroline, then why did you leave?' Rafe took her face in his hands and looked her deeply in the eyes. 'When I discovered the ring by my bedside, I was tempted to come after you, but was afraid. Yesterday I discovered the drawings and looked at them. It was then that I realised you had to care a bit about me, and I realised what a fool I had been for not seeing it, and for letting you go. But I feared I'd left it too late. Then you phoned, and I knew I had to go to you and try.'

'I left because I thought you didn't love me.'

Caroline felt her stomach turn over.

The tears started to well up again and she swallowed hard.

'I couldn't face that, loving you and then having to say goodbye as if I didn't care for you at all. It seemed better that way, cleaner, neater, less painful. After all, the castle had been saved.'

Rafe wiped away a tear from her cheek with his thumb.

'I'd have torn down every stone with my bare hands, if it meant having you instead.'

His husky voice was barely above a whisper.

'But I thought the castle and the estate were the most important things in the world to you,' Caroline began.

Rafe put a finger on her lips.

'Trees, objects and the like are not the most important things. They cannot love you back, only people can. If I didn't know that before, I know that now.'

'You mean you care that much for me that you'd be willing to give up the castle?'

'If it means keeping you, yes, I thought we might be able to live down in London during part of the week, if that's what you feel your business needs. What I am trying to say is that wherever you are, that's where I want to be.'

Caroline put her finger on his lips.

'There is a slight snag to your plans. I won't be in London much longer. I've done a lot of thinking as well. I was wrong to tell you my business could only be located in London. There is a place in Hexham which suits my needs much better. I've spoken with Jules and Margo and they agree. The business is moving up to Northumberland at the end of the month.'

A lump formed in her throat.

'You see . . . I thought . . . we might see each other sometime, and maybe you'd begin to care for me a little.'

'Caroline Adams, you have a choice,' Rafe said seriously after a long moment, holding her away from him.

Caroline's hands started to tremble, and her stomach knotted. She didn't want to think about choices, she wanted to live for this moment.

'There are two people in this room,' he continued, staring directly ahead, 'who could grow old, bitter and twisted with only their thoughts of what could have been, or they could give each other a great deal of happiness, and grow old together, spending each day with the other until their lives ended. It's your choice. I've made mine.'

Caroline took Rafe's face in her hands and turned it towards her.

'I choose life.'

Something heavy slipped on the third finger of her left hand. She looked down and gasped. The sapphire ring, the ring that she had thought when she first saw it should symbolise true love, was on her finger.

'Given to my one and only with all my love,' Rafe said, entwining his hand with hers. 'I had my hopes, you see.'

'And it is accepted with all my love,' Caroline replied, surrendering her lips to his in a long, loving embrace.

We do hope that you have enjoyed reading this large print book.

Did you know that all of our titles are available for purchase?

We publish a wide range of high quality large print books including:
Romances, Mysteries, Classics
General Fiction
Non Fiction and Westerns

Special interest titles available in large print are:
The Little Oxford Dictionary
Music Book, Song Book
Hymn Book, Service Book

Also available from us courtesy of Oxford University Press:
Young Readers' Dictionary
(large print edition)
Young Readers' Thesaurus
(large print edition)

For further information or a free brochure, please contact us at:
Ulverscroft Large Print Books Ltd.,
The Green, Bradgate Road, Anstey,
Leicester, LE7 7FU, England.
Tel: (00 44) **0116 236 4325**
Fax: (00 44) **0116 234 0205**

SUMMER OF LOVE

Christina Jones

It's the summer of 1969: an exciting time of music and fashion, peace and love. However, the Swinging Sixties seem to have by-passed the village of Ashcote. There, 17-year-old Clemmie is thinking only of sitting her A-levels, gaining a place at university and the long, hot summer stretching ahead of her. But when she meets the gorgeous Lewis Coleman-Beck, Clemmie's life changes in a split-second and she is plunged, head-over-heels, into her very own Summer of Love.

THE BLOODSTONE RING

Sara Judge

Edward takes Emma, his betrothed, to visit his Uncle and Aunt Lowther, at Musgrove Manor. Edward adored his uncle's first wife, Aunt Lilian, but she died in childbirth and her two children arc unwanted at Musgrove. When Emma befriends the girls, Margaret, the eldest, is frightened. What is the secret of that odd household? Why does Lilian's ring have a strange effect on Emma when she wears it? Whilst Emma attracts the attention of two bachelors during her stay, she also has to cope with the antagonism of Aunt Prudence Lowther.

WINGS OF THE DOVES

Sheila Lewis

Pilot Alan Ingram achieves his dream when he launches an air charter service on the small Scottish island of Heronsay. He meets opposition from his wife Susan and son Daniel, both reluctant to leave their studies in Glasgow. Daughters Clare, a medical student, and Jessica, on a gap year in Australia, are supportive but have problems of their own. Each member of the family is faced with adversity and doubts about the future, plus the puzzle of a long-lost relative.